P9-CBL-790

Praise for *Chambers of the Heart*

"... stories squarely [in] the literary lineage of James Tiptree and Algis Budrys, the territory where mythmaking and SF intersect. ... remarkably effective stories ... A marvelously varied and heart-tugging collection of tales."

—*Kirkus Reviews, RECOMMENDED*

"...ideally will be read and enjoyed by literary audiences who will relish their metaphorical descriptions, portals to other places and realizations, and the opportunity to juxtapose an eclectic series of themes and experiences into evocative, lovely prose. Literary libraries strong in short fiction and speculative works will find Chambers of the Heart a powerful collection especially highly recommended for discussion groups focused on quick, hard-hitting short stories."

—*D. Donovan, Senior Reviewer, Midwest Book Review, REVIEWER'S CHOICE*

"Each story is a marvel that regards the simple and the grand in beautiful, haunting fashion. ... Allen is highly imaginative, engaging his audience into the otherworldly, and one never knows where the stories lead to or quite what to expect."

—*Dylan Ward, US Review of Books, RECOMMENDED*

"*Chambers of the Heart* is an exceptional collection of stories. Each was more engrossing and inventive than the last. ... lusciously poetic ... rich and vivid ... simultaneously brilliant and devastating ... I loved it with all my heart, and if you only pick up one short story collection this year, make sure it's this one.

—*Writing Werewolf*

"Hauntingly beautiful, engaging, and thoughtful in its approach, author B. Morris Allen's *Chambers of the Heart: speculative stories* is a must-read short story collection of 2022. Thought-provoking narratives which challenge the readers understanding of reality and the emotional character traits to keep the reader invested in each story make this a one-of-a-kind collection that comes along once in a great while."

—*Jack Chambers, Pacific Book Review, STARRED*

"[A] visual, beautiful, heartfelt book that makes you think. ... These stories are powerful and extremely memorable."

—*Amy Lignor, Reader Views*

"*Chambers of the Heart* is an exemplary collection ... I'd highly recommend it to fans of thought-provoking speculative fiction."

—*K.C. Finn, Readers' Favorite*

"beautifully nuanced ... unique and imaginative ... gorgeous prose."

—*Asher Sayed, Readers' Favorite*

"I ended up really loving this collection. It was poignant, heartfelt, and wonderfully crafted."

—*K0pratic, The Fantasy Inn*

"Poignant, heartfelt, and beautifully crafted, *Chambers of the Heart* is an amazing collection of magical and thought-provoking speculative short-stories worthy of savoring and re-reading. ... To successfully incorporate such meaningful depth to the reader in abstract storytelling such as this.... is nothing short of genius. ... Every story in this book is equally memorable."

—*BookeryBliss*

Chambers of the Heart

speculative stories

Also from Metaphorosis

Plant Based Press

Best Vegan Science Fiction & Fantasy
2016-2020

from B. Morris Allen:
Chambers of the Heart: speculative stories
Susurrus
Allenthology: Volume I
Tocsin: and other stories
Start with Stones: collected stories
Metaphorosis: a collection of stories

Verdage

Reading 5X5 x2: Duets
Score – an SFF symphony
Reading 5X5: Readers' Edition
Reading 5X5: Writers' Edition

Metaphorosis Magazine

Metaphorosis: Best of 20xx
Metaphorosis 20xx: The Complete Stories
annual issues, from 2016

Monthly issues

Vestige

The Nocturnals, by Mariah Montoya

Chambers of the Heart

---

speculative stories

B. Morris Allen

ISBN: 978-1-64076-518-4 (e-book)
ISBN: 978-1-64076-519-1 (paperback)
ISBN: 978-1-64076-520-7 (hardcover)

from Metaphorosis Publishing

Neskowin

Contents

Chambers of the Heart

Despair and Ecstasy are the simplest. Ecstasy is the small and cozy room of a cottage that looks out on a broad meadow in the forest. In the spring, elk come to posture and to mate, and the wildflowers bloom on every side. In the fall, mist dances in silver swirls framed by gold and bronze and copper trees. It is always spring or fall.

Despair is a vast, dark hall of low ceilings and small windows. In winter, snowdrifts sometimes cover the windows so that they are only squares of gray against black stone. In the summer, shafts of hot, bright light do nothing to warm the room, and only blind us to the room's darkness, so that we must carry candles to the Master's hard throne. It is always winter or summer.

Ecstasy and Despair are the simplest chambers, and the worst, and they are where the Master spends his time.

Today, though, I am pleased to find him in the low hall of Longing. He sits by the fire, a book spread open on one leg, his eyes on the soft river of cloud beyond the window, and the shining peaks in the distance.

"Sunset is beautiful," he says. "The way it paints the snow of distant mountains with ..."

"With crimson?" I suggest. It is always sunset in the hall of Longing, but our Master is no poet.

"With crimson." He sighs, and raises his book. "The poet Lanoy said that 'the sun's bright ardor brings a blush and a glow to the earth's shy breasts'. It sounds better in Clanetian, but I fear Lanoy was a man desperately in need of a lover. He should not have become a monk." He puts the book back down. I have never seen him read it.

"*Would* that I had a lover," the Master says. His latest has just left him. I can see one fist clenching, the fingers working deep furrows in his thigh. I go to stand beside him, as if my presence could deflect him from his course.

"Please, Master," I beg. "Don't go again into Despair." He has spent the past weeks in that dark hall, slumped in its hard stone chair, punishing himself and us. Better Ecstasy than that.

"No," he says, and his grip relaxes. I imagine the welts beneath his cotton trousers, the bruises they will leave. "I must distract myself," he says. "I will go to the theater. I will talk, I will laugh, I will smile." He gazes out again, across the blushing peaks. "And yet, I wish I had someone to laugh with. Someone to smile at. Ah, well. We cannot have all we want."

He is safe now, I think, and I go to prepare a meal. I will find him again in the hall of Longing, or in some byway near it, perhaps, in an alcove of Yearning, or a gallery of Ache.

As I climb the narrow backstairs, I pass other servants, all quiet and intent on their errands, as I am on mine. We seldom speak, and I do not know their names. As I pass behind the walls of Satisfaction, my foot slips, and a chambermaid reaches out to catch me. I draw my hand away, ashamed, but she is as old as I, and there is no pity in her gaze. Her hair is gray, like the clouds of Longing, and as I look upon it her eyes widen. I wonder what she sees. I open my mouth to speak, but then I turn away. I am an old man now. In my youth, I kept my passions in check, until they left me for other, wilder spirits. The maid and I go our ways in silence.

I eat my meal in silence, in the warm staff kitchen, at the little table that is always set. With the Master lost in the ways of Distraction, I have time. I watch the cooks as they do their quiet work. One stirs a pot of stew — a tasty concoction of roots and sharp spices. He jokes quietly with a flour-handed baker stoking her oven. It warms my soul to see them. The young so often waste their youth, and I have myself for an example. These two are wiser now than I ever was. They are shy to have an audience, but I see their looks, hear their soft laughter, and I rise to leave them be.

I make my leisurely way down toward Longing, but though I have gone slowly, the Master is not here. I wait for some time, and even make the long descent to Despair, but he is not there, though I search its darkness with careful steps, quartering back and forth with my dim candle across its obsidian floor.

I climb the steep stairs back from Despair, but Longing is bare, and I do not hear or feel him near. I know what this must mean, and I am tempted to stop, to rest, to wait. To fail. But I have served the

Master all my life; it is my life. My duty will not cease because I am tired or selfish.

I climb the long, gentle ramp from Longing to Fulfillment, passing through and past rooms of Relaxation and Relief. I wonder idly, as I pass through Tranquility and Quietude, whether the old chamber maid cleans these rooms, whether some day we will pass again in one chamber or another. Perhaps we have often done so.

The Master is not in Fulfillment, but I knew that, and though it is the most beautiful of chambers, I pass through its moonlit wooden chairs, with barely a glance through the windows to its quiet dawn-flecked lake. No, the Master was in Longing, and he has gone out to company. If he has not returned to Longing or to Despair, there is only one place he can be, and I pass on.

The Master stands by the wood-framed window of Ecstasy, his narrow frame bathed in sweat, a smile across his face like the rictus of lockjaw.

"Oh, but the world is a beautiful place," he says to the wildflower bouquets of spring. "The colors, the rush of life, the flow of nature's grace." He shakes his head, but his smile is fixed, and no mere shake will dislodge it. "What have I done, I wonder, to deserve such happiness?"

That way lies Despair, and I know, with the certainty of experience, that this interlude of Ecstasy will be a brief one. "Do not say that, Master. You, as no other, deserve happiness." I try, but I know he will not listen, cannot listen to other than the voices in his head that tell him otherwise.

"He is so beautiful," he says. "A dancer, lithe as a willow, strong as an oak. He could pick me up with one strong hand. He did so!"

“You are a lucky man, Master. And strong in ways that he is not.” I know he does not listen.

“What could he see in me, I wonder?” As he speaks, he wipes himself with a soft towel, leaves it to dry on the arm of a chair. The chambermaids will find it. “A frail reed with little to offer. A poor artist. A dreadful poet with the voice of a crow.” He is already on his way to the door.

“A good man,” I insist, though the tears have already started in my eyes. “A hard worker, and a kind master.” Doomed to bounce endlessly from Despair to Ecstasy and back, and only because he is not strong or handsome or, in fact, very wise. But he is gentle and caring and honest, and someday, if he can only muster confidence, he will find a man who values that.

Now, though, I can hear him in the passage. “It is no wonder he has not come to call,” he says, and then his voice fades, and I must rush to follow. The Master has his own ways, fast and sure and painful, but I can only scurry and stumble through the long halls and stairs and byways toward Despair.

In the narrow path of Desperation, I run headlong into the old chambermaid. She catches me again before we both fall. “You must not make this a habit,” I say, and am shocked to find such wit in my dry mouth. But my courage fails as she drops my arm, and I realize that my tongue has failed me, that in so many dour and taciturn years, it has lost the knack for banter, has rendered my poor jest harsh and bitter.

My face settles back into its familiar, comfortable lines, all angles and ridges. I see the shine in her eyes vanish, but it lingers in the soft silver bird's nest of her hair, and I grasp for something to say. "I am Akro," I say. "The Master's Ear."

"I know," she says, and moonlight glimmers in the windowless passage. "I am Lucy." And she rushes away.

It is as well, for the Master needs me, and I must scamper on my way, but even in these dark lower stairs and alcoves, my heart is light. For once, Despair holds no dread for me, and I walk with a quick step toward the Master's cold throne.

"He has not called on me," he says at once. "And he has been seen at the Berry Wreath with Lord Consany — half my age, and broad as an ox. But no brighter." He turns his eyes toward the glare of a summer window, and the light shows the tracks of tears down his face.

"You are intelligent, Master," I say, because it is true. There is no sign that he has heard me. There is never a sign. "And gracious, and thoughtful."

He looks out the window to the burning sun beyond, and out of habit, I warn him not to look, to mind his eyes.

He wipes a hand over his eyes, smearing the shadows he painted there to make his pale eyes luminous and rich. "I will never be happy," he says, and begins to sob. It is my task to listen, not to speak. I have spent my life listening.

"Not if you act like a child," I say, and wonder how my tongue, earlier so cold and clumsy, has suddenly become so sharp. "You are a good man, Master, but you seek what you will never find. You eat rich foods and complain of belly pain. You contest at sports you cannot win. You love young men who want only to play." You talk with those who cannot hear.

“What is this?” The Master has a card in his hand. “He has come!” He throws himself from his chair, and I hear his laughter dwindling as he makes his rapid way to Ecstasy.

I set my foot on the stair from Despair, to follow, to listen, to be my Master's Ear, as I always have been, as I always will be. And yet, I wonder as I climb the dark steps, whether the Master might be better served by absence, whether, without a willing Ear, he might be forced to listen for himself, and whether, doing so, he might hear something.

As I pass through the low hall of Longing, I gaze across its sun-lit mountain peaks and remember youth. I turn away from the window's rosy lure, and climb the long, gentle ramp. I will wander the hallways above until I see the glint of bright eyes and silver hair. Then, if she is willing, we will enter my favorite chamber, and stand together in the gentle light of dawn.

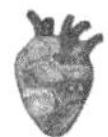

About the story

I have a very minor heart condition. Confirming its nature required a day wearing a heart monitor, which naturally had me thinking about the heart and its chambers. I wondered what life in those chambers might be like if they were neither biological nor purely metaphorical, but an actual residence. The opening line came quickly after that, and with just a little tweaking to decide on seasons and views, the main elements were in place. I had the idea that the master inhabits the rooms, but that he never clearly interacts with his servants, and that his dialogue with his principal servant could just as well be a monologue.

It's a somewhat odd piece, but I had fun with it, and it emerged fairly quickly. I liked the ending's focus on fulfillment rather than the master's constant, fruitless chase of ecstasy.

Building on Sand

He had been ready; a small bag packed, boots oiled, axe sharpened. He had meant to go, but he had not gone.

He could remember the feel of it still, the sense of a burden lifted, of freedom at last in his grasp. It had felt ... lonely, in a way; frightening. Before, he had had his task, his role, his definition. In that brief moment of independence, those certainties had gone, vanished like rain seeping into sand, leaving just a damp, irritating grit behind.

It rubbed now, between the thick calluses of duty, and the fragile fabric of hope, worn thin as memory. Soon enough, that fabric would tear, and he would have to admit at last that only useless rags remained.

He had had a plan. For years, decades even, he had had a plan. First, it had been simply to return — to love, to Anoush, to *home,* whatever that might be. To serve his time in the Sand Guard with honor, and then go back to making carpets, his life-tax paid, his obligations all fulfilled. By then, Anoush would have finished her own time in the salt ponds, would be back laying clay pipe for the town's plumbing. They would live happily ever after. Maybe a child, maybe not, as fate might have it. They would expand the gardens, and he would clear out that area behind the workshop and make it into a lawn where he and his workers would play with his dogs in the mist of Anoush's new-built fountain. He could still feel the cool of the spray on his cheek, the warmth of a dog's muzzle resting on his thigh.

He had almost made it. Had gotten as far as the high hills, far enough to see Kellno's white-slate roofs gleaming in the distance, like a waypoint in the valley's grey floor, a stepping stone to contentment.

But then the once-a-century green rains had come, and the forest had grown, trees edging in against the sand moats like maggots in a wound. That had been the turning point, probably. He could have gone on. His service had been done, his obligations met. And yet, if the forest encroached, if it brought its evil across the moats, if the twisting roots of its looming giants once met those of the lower, more modest local trees, what value would there be in home? What love would he find, in his gardens and his lawn, as bright and bilious green leaves began to arch overhead, to leave his life and love in shade?

And so he had turned back, had climbed back down the hills, back over the mountain to Cyla, with its mansions and towers and proximity to the sand belt. He had walked back into the barracks, and the sergeant there had asked no questions, only pointed him back at his bunk, moved his name chit back into rotation, reissued him his axe.

All these years, he'd had the same axe. He'd never even broken the handle, never replaced the head, had avoided the metaphysical trap of identity that his colleagues batted around at noon-time discussions. It was the same axe. He wished he could say the same for himself.

They'd fought back the forest, and the green rains had gone back to whatever hell they came from, and the canton was safe. But somehow, in the crisis, he had rescued a family from an oasis gone bad, a pleasant verdance gone vile and vicious, had brought them safely back to clean pure sand. Not just him. They all had saved people, every one of them. Marta, who had given her life to take down a red-barked leaf-dropper to save a cluster of sheep that had hidden, panicked, under the false shelter of its boughs. She had cut it through, by herself, before it could spray its cruel, clinging pollen, and turn soft fleece into a foul imitation of woodland, and its hosts to carrion. She had used her own weight to force the tree to fall back, despite its reaching, clinging branches. He had stayed only long enough to see the rootlets growing into her, through her, and to chop off her head.

And Halek, who had thrown fox cubs across a stream to where their mother waited, anxious, and had barely leapt across himself before the pine cones began exploding and a makeshift wall of fence pickets barred his way. And Ruba, and Nizrah. They had all saved people.

Why, then, had his burden been so much heavier? Why had Elya and Ramzi clung so firmly to him, once rescued, depended on him so thoroughly?

Their home had been destroyed, of course, their oasis, once a clear watering hole of bright flowers and soft breezes, reduced by the Sand Guard to a smoldering pile of coal and mud. They had had dogs and children to feed, and no prospect of work, with Elya's limited mobility, and Ramzi's bad vision. And so, of course, he had stayed, had written to Anoush and assured her that it would a matter of a few months.

She had understood, had waited, as months turned into years, as Elya and Ramzi's children grew up, and their dogs grew old and sick, needing care. He'd taken other work, by then, first as a woodman, then as trainer with the Sand Guard, then as recordsman. And before Elya's eldest Lara had earned her journeyman status and a wage the family could live on, Anoush had written again.

She loved him still, but age brought with it decisions, and she wanted children, and she would invite Darl to live with her — gentle, friendly Darl against whom nothing could be said — unless he came home this year, and how she wished he would. And Darl had sent his own note to say how sweet Anoush remained, and how she loved him despite his absence, and how he should come back now, and toss duty to the wind.

And then Ramzi's eldest dog had died, and the next one soon to go, and Lara had set aside her apprenticeship to mourn with her parents, even though it meant a year's delay, and a break with her own lover.

And so he had blessed Anoush and Darl, and had stayed, and fed his second family. His only family, now. And when at last Lara made journeyman, and Lirl did, and Kerigo opened a shop and got married, he stayed on in Cyla. Still strong, still able, a middle-aged man at loose ends. He had tried to open a carpet mill, but the beauty of the work had faded, the patterns just mechanical abstractions now, the quality a matter of work, and no longer of pride. He had sold it at a loss within a year, and taken work as a steward instead, a job with clear boundaries and few decisions that really mattered.

He had sent his wages back to Anoush and Darl, along with advice about carpets, and delight in Anoush's innovations in pipefitting. He had sent sincere congratulations about their baby, and kept his pain and heartbreak to himself, tending it carefully, until it formed a rich compost for love and devotion to the child, Ara.

They'd exchanged messages over the years, and he'd sent gifts — little trinkets from the big city, as if Cyla were the distant capital, instead of a built-up border post with a river. And in time Ara himself had married, and named the boy Peno, after him, though the spelling was simpler, more modern. He had wanted to go back, then, to take up his role as uncle and ... something.

But then there had been that ill-considered insurrection, and the canton had mobilized to root out traitors, and his employer had panicked about some shady payments and equally shady friends. She had needed her level-headed steward to save her from herself, and her family from her foolishness. And so he had stood, axe in hand, at the house's door, and his old friend Halek had led the team that came to turn them out. They had talked, and Halek had trusted him, and turned away. His employer, who had talked of bags of gold, had given him a handful of silver and a sack of promises. But her daughter, who was only a baby, and liked to play with the kitten, had given him a smile.

For the sake of that smile, he had stayed, until the hubbub had died down, and the roads were safe to travel again, and Anoush had died.

The will had gone out of him, then, and no matter that Darl had written, and Ara, begging him to come back, he had stayed, and sent a bag of silver for the town plumbing fund, and cried while he watched the baby and she touched his tears and laughed her burbly laugh, and the kitten climbed to his shoulder and licked his cheek dry with a tiny, raspy tongue.

Ara had come to see him, then — a slight, warm-eyed man who talked about his mother, and her love for his other father, for so he called him. And Pënho had told the boy stories of their youth, and of Anoush's grand dreams of cisterns and sewers. They had all come true, Ara said, all but her grandest dream of all. And they had both cried, and agreed that Darl was a good man, and a fine carpet maker, and that Pënho would come home soon.

He had given his notice, once the harvest was in and stored and sent to market, and the fields prepared for winter. And then it was winter, and it was cold, and he found to his surprise that he could no longer stand the long nights and hard road when he made his trips to arrange the sales and the workforce for sewing time. And so he stayed until spring, though word came that Darl had taken ill.

In the spring, as soon as a morning came without frost, he gave warning again. His employer accepted it without question, and agreed to keep on the apprentice he'd trained up from the kitchen staff.

He had packed up a small bag, and sharpened his axe in case of bandits, and oiled his new canvas boots in case of mud, and he had gone to say his goodbyes.

The baby was talking clearly now, and no longer really a baby at all. He hugged her tight when the nurse had gone, and kissed her on the forehead, and blew a raspberry there until she laughed.

"I'm going now," he told her when he put her down.

"To see Peno," she said, serious.

"That's right," he said.

"But you're not his granddaddy," she said, brow furrowed as she tried to work out relations that were well beyond her.

"Not really," he admitted with a smile. "But sort of."

"You're not my granddaddy either," she said with indisputable logic.

"No." Though he had tried to be, with the father gone, the mother busy, and the real grandparents far away.

"Then why don't you stay with me?" she asked. "We can play hide and seek." She put a hand over her eyes to show him how the game worked.

He passed a hand over his own eyes and smiled softly. "I'd like to," he said. "We have fun, don't we? But Peno needs me."

"I need you," she said. "I need you too. For when kitten gets her claw caught in the blanket and she can't get it out. And when I fall down and my knee hurts, and you have to kiss it. And when you cry and you don't want anyone to see it," she said, and traced a tear down his furrowed cheek. "And you don't even know Peno."

He had made his choice then, reached the second turning point, and once again turned back, as he had so many years before. Was it duty, he wondered now, or cowardice? Was he stepping up to take his place, to make his small contribution to the bulwark against evil, or was he hunkering down, digging for what small shelter he could find against the green verge of terror and uncertainty?

Peno was Ara's son, and Anoush's grandson, and Darl's. He'd never met the boy, and it suddenly came to him just how fragile was the structure of family he'd built up in his thoughts, how little foundation it had in reality. Oh, they'd tried to include him, had reached out farther than logic could support, as far as love could reach. They had done their best, and he didn't doubt that Ara cared for him; his visit showed as much. He didn't doubt that Peno had heard of him, had dreamed his own childish dreams of meeting this name from the past, reinforced now by Ara's stories and descriptions. They would be fast friends, no doubt. He smiled at the thought, at the image of them both on the lawn, covered in Ara's dogs, their snouts digging under arms and elbows to reach the hidden faces, to cover them with licks and love.

And if he didn't go, didn't make the hard journey, didn't take his bag, and his boots, and his shining axe? Peno would miss him; might even cry, one day, at the loss of the playmate he'd been promised. And then he would go on, would forget, would lose himself in a pile of furry friends who would lick dry the tears, and turn them to giggles and to hugs.

Ara would miss him, but Ara could come again, some day, with a load of carpets and contracts. And Darl? Darl was a good man, no doubt. He had been a good father, a good grandfather, a good businessman. He had made Anoush happy. For that, Pënho owed him. But perhaps that debt was paid, already, had been paid in years and tears of absence, of non-interference. Had been paid by not breaking up his happiness, by letting him live his life as best he could, with the family he had made without Pënho's help.

And here? Here was a little girl neglected by her mother, brought up by maids and nannies, and a kitten, and by one stooped, grizzled old steward who played hide and seek, and held her when she cried, and when he did, and who loved her, he realized, as he had loved nothing else in his life that was solid and tangible. And if that was less than he had loved dreams and hopes and distance, it was still love, and it was still real.

He had thought it was duty that caused him to turn back in his tracks, and perhaps once it had been. Obligation to his country, to his people, to his future. But, now, he had no duties, had met his charges, done his work, filled his role. Now, when he looked in his dreams, there was no future, no need to put off happiness until the future — there was only now, only a small girl, and a kitten, and a warmth in his heart. The fabric of hope wore gradually away, and he felt it go, felt it pull away, leaving him cushioned by a quiet contentment and the knowledge that for the moment, at least, there was only himself to think of.

He unpacked his small bag, now, and set his oiled boots in the little niche under his shelves. The axe he wrapped carefully in oiled cloth, and then in waxed cotton, and leaned carefully in the back corner of his room, to remind him of darker, stronger days, when duty and service had been his mainstays, and his shield against pain and loss. But his days of toil and trouble were done, and the axe would stay where it was. Perhaps some day Ara would take it away as a puzzling gift to Peno from the non-grandfather he would never know, and never really miss.

In soft slippers, with a hitch in his step, and a small cargo of love in his heart, he left his room and walked down to the nursery, to cry with his small friend, and play hide and seek with her while she forgot that he had ever thought to leave.

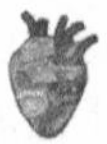

About the story

I happened on an animated film of *The Little Prince* (2015, directed by Mark Osborne). All I recall now is that it involved a young girl getting to know an older neighbour. However, I know that the relationship triggered in me the idea of a story about an older person who has to leave a place, out of an obligation to his child. Instead, he stays to keep another child company. The story that emerged stayed largely on target, though I found they inhabited an interesting world.

Blush

I've been down in the heart of Wrinkletown, stood in the Blemish itself, with unmasked people as far as the eye can see. You get used to it. Eventually, you realize that wrinklies aren't so bad. In fact, they're just like normal people — just more open about it.

"Oh, Saja, it was awful. They took him out of the autowomb and just *showed* him to us! Can you imagine?" My heart raced at the memory — the plumdark prune where a face should have been, all creases and crinkles and corrugation. "It was like packing material. Dirty packing material."

"Ew." A slight tightening of the eyes showed her distaste. Saja's facial masking emphasized curves and exaggerated her features — a deliberate rejection of the fashion for flat planes and minimalized noses. "Which one of you did he look like?" A smile flickered past lush, graceful lips

"Funny." As if I would know. I'd never seen myself without masking, let alone Brendan. "We were pretty shaken up."

"I can imagine, Jene." Saja's color was a delicate mauve on the cheeks, deepening to rich brownish clay on the temples and brow. I wondered whether she'd give me the design. Probably not. She's paid to be a trend-setter, and I'm as far from trends as you can get. "I hear babies look like something out of Wrinkletown." The city's twelfth district, set aside for those disturbed souls who chose to go unmade. "He looks normal enough now, anyway."

We looked at the cradlebot, just inserting a nipple between my son's plump red lips. He took it with a happy gurgle.

"Yes, well, the nurse took him and gave him to the smoother right away. There's a job I wouldn't take." The mere thought was repulsive. "Looking at unmade babies all day long. A whole day of it. It's awful."

"Someone has to do it. Be thankful it's not you."

"I suppose. Though with the amount we paid for gene-mods, you'd think he'd have just been born...you know...presentable."

"All's well that ends well." She glanced over at the cradle where Enrique's cheeks glowed with carefully applied good health. "Is this his look?"

Was that a touch of condescension? Brendan and I had chosen a conservative look, one we felt could last for years before redesign. Was it too traditional, too boring? "We thought it would work initially," I said with caution.

"Oh yes. He looks fine. Very 'I'm a baby.' " I winced. "Whenever you do decide to update, let me know if you want me to take a look."

Brendan and I had argued about that point when she made her first offer, before the birth. Brendan was in sales, and thought we didn't need some 'celeb' giving us tips. I told him there was no call to be nasty, and it all got worse from there.

"Thanks, sis. Will do."

"Not that he doesn't look good now. Traditionalism is making a comeback."

"How's business?" Anything to change the subject.

"Good!" A gentle smile curled the tips of her mouth at just the right angle. "Krasiv & Bella just sent me their latest kit — reaches all the way around the head. It can even redistribute follicles, see?" She turned to show me the back of her neck. It looked long and bare and just the same as always.

"Very nice."

"A little painful, but ..." She shrugged and rose. "Anyway. I have to go." She leaned down to kiss my brow. "And turn down the gloss a little on your eyeshine maybe?" She winked; friendly advice to the dowdy brother, no offense intended.

"Bye, Saj. Thanks for listening." Saja wasn't much of a listener, but I'd had to tell *someone*, and it wasn't the kind of story you could share with colleagues or casual acquaintances. "My moment in the dark ages." When people had walked around with faces naked for everyone to see, forcing each other to stare at every blotch and bruise and birthmark. Birthmarks! The very concept was grotesque.

"Maybe it'll grow on you. Next I see you, you'll be a full-fledged wrinkly," she teased, and closed the door behind her.

A wrinkly. I shuddered, telling the housebot to clear the dishes. Could anyone really go out in public unmade? They couldn't legally, of course; not outside Wrinkletown. But who would have the courage, even there, among other wrinklies?

The whole idea made me faintly nauseous, and I stepped into my prepper. The door closed and locked firmly, and I turned the manual lock as well. The solid thunk of the bolt was reassuring — snug in my own little well of privacy, safe from peering eyes and cameras and recorders, without judges other than myself, and that was plenty. The telltales in the mirror glowed green to confirm my seclusion.

I slid onto the little stool, leaned my face into the soft mask of the painter. No fancy wraparound model here — just a dependable, high-end conservative model with a hair attachment. Saja had programmed it for me, initially, but I had toyed with the parameters a little. Too much, perhaps. I dialed down the eyeshine a little. The avatar looked dull, and I added a little blue to compensate. That fit poorly with my loamy skin tone. I played with options for a while, steadily making matters worse.

"Just wipe it," I said in frustration. "No!" I closed my eyes just as the avatar turned a dull khaki, the nose too big, the lips too thin. "Apply Saja 1," I said hurriedly. The design was a good two years old, but Saja was a leader, not a follower. The design might be dated, but it would still work.

All through the afternoon, as I outlined a report for the desk to write, I was distracted by the specter of a coarse nose hulking above lips like dry planks. Was that how I looked? When the outline was done, the desk compiling, I sought solace in cookery, ignoring the house's predicted match in favor of creativity. I chose basil, zucchini, seitan, buckwheat, played with spices and cooking styles until I had something novel, and scheduled it to cook.

It was a disaster, of course. Brendan had had a long day of meetings, negotiating new water rights for the Gorge. I could see the irritation in his eyes, the slight flush that even his careful masking couldn't hide. He looked across the artful table of grilled and toasted delicacies and told the house to make him a sandwich.

"How's the baby?" he asked, making conversation as the house slid a perfectly toasted sandwich in front of him — dark rye with zucchini and seitan strips. We both stared at it until he forced a smile.

"Fine. Eats well. Sleeps well." I strove for something less anodyne. "Saj was by. She says hello." She'd said no such thing, and he knew it.

"Give her my love." He quirked a perfect eyebrow to share the joke, declare a truce.

"Bren," I blurted, knowing the moment was wrong. "Have you ever wondered what you look like?"

"I know exactly-"

"No, not your face. I mean, beneath the face. What you really look like." In for a penny. "Unmade."

The false cheer drained from the smooth white of his face. "Is this about the baby? The attendant's been fired, the nurse penalized. There's nothing more to think about."

"No. Yes. I don't know. I just..." What did I? "I was just curious, is all. In the prepper today, I -"

"What you do in the prepper is for you to think about." Evidently marriage only took us so far. "Look, Jene." The epitome of reasonableness. "Maybe we should reconsider talking to someone. It's a ... a shock, seeing a baby like that. No one should have to see their own son without cosmetics. I can understand if it's ... troubling you."

"Yes, fine. But that's not the point. I ..." I decided to leave it alone. "I'm fine." And I would be. It had been a moment's curiosity, that was all.

"If you're sure." He took a bite of sandwich, wiped a smear of oil from his cheek. The masking self-repaired, showing just a trace of dark stubble before it vanished again under a surface of serene porcelain.

Over the next few weeks, the mental images persisted, and I spent hours looking at my carefully programmed face in the prepper, running a gentle finger over a nose that looked perfectly average. Occasionally, I played a game of chicken with the painter, giving careless commands to wipe my masking, closing my eyes just as the avatar cleared, knowing that some day I would slip, would see again the face beneath my face — my real face, I began to call it.

I confided one day in Saja, with a wince that my masking surely transformed into a glance of mild concern.

"And why shouldn't you?" she asked. "Have you never seen yourself naked?"

"Well, naked, yes." I was reasonably fit for my age. "But ..."

"Unmade is the same. There's no need to be ashamed, Jene, unless you go out in public." She pursed lips now painted a pale blue that contrasted sharply with translucent black skin. "Even that, if you want."

"Oh, come on, Saj. I just asked -"

"Well, why shouldn't you go out unmade, if you want to?"

"Hold on, now. I'm not a wrinkly. I'm just curious."

"No reason you shouldn't be." She leaned forward. "I've done it too."

"Gone out! Surely not."

"Well, not that, no. But I've looked at myself in the prepper."

"Oh." It seemed tame, in contrast. "And?"

She smiled her perfect smile. "Not so bad."

"Really!"

"Really. Wrinkly, of course. Spotted, even. I have," she winked, "freckles. Real ones." They'd been in fashion five years back.

"Really? How did you... What do you look like?"

"Want to see?"

"No! That's... You're my sister!"

"It's not sexual, Jene."

It wasn't, but it was revolting, wrong. And enticing.

"Maybe I'll try it myself," I said to move things along. In the privacy of my prepper.

"You should." She patted my hand, brown masking on black. "Maybe you're a redhead."

I laughed. We'd always mocked the kids who tested the edges of fashion, aimed to shock with extreme looks. I'd kept my own hair within a narrow range of brown for years.

"I'll let you know."

Over the next month, I spent more and more time in the prepper, taking longer and longer glimpses of my unmade avatar. Eventually, I came to moment I had dreaded and anticipated.

"Wipe it," I said firmly. The avatar obligingly faded to its now familiar dingy khaki color, the nose a jutting promontory, the lips a mere suggestion of arc. "Remove masking," I said, with slightly less certainty. The image blanked as the painter began its weekly cleansing. I felt my skin tingle as the layers peeled, as exfoliants scrubbed on, wiped off. I felt raw, exposed, and I waited unconsciously for the gentle, soothing cream base that presaged a fresh masking. It didn't come. I'd set no new painting program. I breathed deep and leaned back.

"No masking applied," warned the screen, flashing red — black — red as I lifted my face, eyes still closed. The air felt cold on my cheeks, and I felt fragile, as if a puff of breath could sear me, mark me, leave a scar to buff away.

I sat, uncertain, with the bright lights of the prepper forcing their way through my eyelids to set violet stains growing, shifting, merging, fading to lilac. Was I ready to face the mirror? Could I face my raw self, my impurities exposed at last, my dark secret thoughts evident to a passing glance? I snapped my eyes open before I could consider further.

It was ... coarse. The skin, a light oatmeal mix of mushroom flecked with sand, was pitted and mined with gross pores, shot through with light blue canals of blood beneath the marbled surface. The nose was a sharp spine terminating in a flat tip with huge, gaping nostrils. Pale blue irises peered out of dingy white mapped in thin red threads. At the outer corners, nets of skin gathered tight against encroaching age. My hair was a weave of dark auburn mixed with dusty grey.

It was crude, like an artist's base, before the final surface was applied. Yet it looked like me. Not the me I was accustomed to seeing, the one that Brendan kissed good night, the one that had greeted my squalling, crinkled son, but a me that felt like me. It smiled when I smiled — a full-face symphony of motion, the lips crooked unevenly, the pale eyes narrowed and wrinkled, the cheeks folding into a relief of thin seams and joints — a far cry from the sleek, subtle aspect I showed the world. It was genuine, majestic, and its ruined beauty cut me to the quick. A tear trembled in one eye, and I blinked, but no masking wicked it away unseen. It trickled wet and cold down a maze of obstacles, turning left at this lump, right at that chasm, to finish at my upper lip, with its dark speckles of shaved but shadowed hair. I touched the moisture with one finger, marveled at the delicate sensitivity of bare lips, tasted salt, felt it drying on my cheek.

"Brendan will arrive in twenty minutes," announced the house. Its cold, matter-of-fact tone broke the spell, left me staring not at an exquisite portrait of Truth, but at a wrinkly — a coarse-featured gargoyle, weathered and withered by exposure.

I plunged my face back into the kit. "Saja 2," I blurted. By the time Brendan opened the door, I was the Jene he knew and loved — as much the real me as anything he'd ever seen. He kissed my full, smooth lips, and all was well.

"My kit broke the other day," Saja said.

I shrugged. Cosmetic companies delivered kits to her every week to endorse, review, occasionally excoriate.

"I went out," she said. I shrugged again. "*Out*," she repeated.

"Oh! You mean..."

"Unmade. Down the street and back."

"Isn't that... Isn't that a risk? I mean..." It's not against the law to go unmade, so long as you stick to walled districts. Wrinkletown. The name tasted stale, unwholesome.

"I met two friends. They congratulated my bold new look." She smiled, delighted. "One asked for the program."

"You could start a new trend." Here was a way forward! "Call it something clever, give out a null program."

"Say it automatically individualizes the look," she agreed. "It would be fun, wouldn't it?"

"Yes! What could we call it? 'Natural', or 'Fresh', or ..."

"Nude."

"I love it! Look, let's -" I stopped, regarded her calm mask, now of pale jasper with hair of jet. "You don't mean it, do you?"

"Really sell the program?" She shrugged. "It would be fun, but it wouldn't go far. There's no real money in it. Besides, what if it caught on?"

"What if it did?"

"Oh Jene, I'm sorry. You're really caught up in this, aren't you? Be serious. I went out for twenty minutes, unmade, and already my skin changed color. I could feel it burning. The next day, I had more freckles than before. Imagine, if I did that every day!" She shook her head. "In any case, how would I change my look? You wouldn't want to look the same every day, would you? I mean, most people wouldn't. And if I did, who would follow me? Who would pay me?"

We left it at that. I said no more about my experimentation, my weekly self-examination. I scheduled my weeklies now when Brendan was at the office. We no longer engaged in our morning ritual of mutual appraisal, our small efforts to surprise each other, to deserve the minor compliments we gave each other more now by rote than out of interest. We focused instead on Enrique, with no better result.

"Look, Jene," Brendan said at last, exasperated. "I understand if you want to make yourself grotesque, wandering around with scarcely any masking. At least you work from home. But the baby is another question. Look at him!"

We looked down at a wriggling, burbling child, eyes bright as he grabbed at a toy dangled by the cradlebot, tried to stuff the toy's smooth plastic into pudgy cheeks mottled with healthy pink. A thin layer of saliva smeared down his double chin.

"He's beautiful."

"He's not! He's a freak! When I wanted to show a picture of him the other day, I had to have the desk doctor one up, so he'd look partway normal. Anila Bates from network ads asked if he was sick!"

"He's perfectly healthy."

"I know he is. But *look* at him."

"I have. Have you, Brendan? Have you ever seen your son without his masking?"

His face, for once so mobile, froze. "What have you been doing, Jene?"

"Looking at our son the way he is. It's not illegal, Brendan."

"Maybe not. But it's not normal, Jene. It has to stop. *You* have to stop. Look, I want you to talk to Saja. She says she started you off on this. Maybe she can bring you back."

Silence. "You talked with Saja?" I asked at last.

"Yes! I'm worried about you, Jene." A trace of the man I married peeked out through the margins of his masking, and my heart warmed. This was the man I'd given my heart. "It's getting so that we can't go anywhere. People might see you." And this was not.

"I can fix that," I answered stiffly, and took my righteous anger to the solitude of the prepper. Inside, I took off my masking, and watched tears flow slowly down my face, leaving slick, salty trails to show their passing. After an hour, Brendan knocked and called my name. I watched my reflection in the mirror as, calmly, serenely, it didn't answer. Eventually he went away.

The next day, Enrique and I, masked in matching sepia skin with chestnut hair, went out. We hailed a cab, directed it to the edge of the twelfth district, near a cafe I liked. It was a thin pretense, if Brendan checked the charges, but it was something. Enrique strapped tight to my chest, I walked down one block to the walls that marked off Wrinkletown. A guard stood at the edge, but he did no more than give us a 'takes all kinds' look as we passed in. His function was to prevent the unmade from coming out.

'Welcome to Wrinkletown!' offered a bright, tattered sign. 'Be yourself.' The streets were dirty, as if they saw only occasional cleaning. I watched a crumpled candy wrapper flutter down the street before circling at a corner and settling in the gutter.

Above it, a sign offered fresh juice, and I walked toward it.

The proprietor was a wrinkly, or near one. He wore a thin layer of masking, perhaps hiding minor blots, but doing nothing to disguise a lump on the side of his nose, or an imperfectly shaven cheek.

"Morning," he said sceptically. "Help you?"

"Some juice, please. Uh, grapefruit." I couldn't keep my eyes off him, off the uneven stubble that dangled from his gaunt left cheek, so different from the smooth, equally gaunt right one. So flawed; so public.

He nodded. One long, unshaven hair waggled slightly with the motion.

"Here you go," he said, sliding a scratched but immaculately clean glass across the counter. a paper-wrapped straw beside it. "Don't get a lot of kids in with the gawpers," he nodded at Enrique. "Training him young, are you?"

"What?" Gawpers. He meant me. "No! No, not gawping. I ..." How could I explain to a stranger my perverse prepper habits?

"Ah." He looked more closely at my masking, and I could feel the thin cover falling apart under the sheer pressure of his gaze. I wanted to touch my cheek, see if the flakes were already starting to peel off, or if it was coming off in long sheets that would dangle off my chin like wattles. "Welcome, then," he said more warmly. He nodded at the baby again. "He's welcome too."

"Thanks." I sipped my juice, through a straw, since the acid strips away lipmask. "How... do you..." I waved a hand in vague indication.

"Get along?" He smiled, a great chasm of cheer that showed rough lips and yellowed teeth. "Well enough." He waved out the window. "The services don't ever seem to come on time, mind you, and to buy the good stuff, we have to mask up and go out. But well enough, aside from that."

"Is it ... hard?"

He knew I wasn't asking about shopping. "Not a bit of it. It's comfortable, in a way, always seeing faces you know, recognize. Love. And they do change, you know."

"Age." Wrinkles, spots, signs of decay.

"Age. Wrinkles and blotches. Slumps and stoops. Wisdom and experience. Laughter and learning. It's not for everyone." He appraised me, shrugged. "Maybe not you."

Was I to be rejected so quickly, before I had even started? A part of me felt immense relief at this reprieve from imagined, predicted battles. The vocal part objected. "Maybe. Maybe it is me."

He looked at me again, at Enrique, pudgy limps dangling, a thread of drool just starting to drip down his fat neck to be absorbed by masking. "Tell you what. Take this." He slipped a thin leaflet from a box on the counter. "Take it home. Read it. Think about it. If you want to, check it out."

I took the leaflet, held it in sweaty hands. 'The Naked Truth,' it read. 'Life without masks.' There was an address in the twelfth district.

"Keep that private," the man advised. "Best that way. If you come back, the office is on the Blemish — the square." He smiled. "Tell them Jose sent you." He offered a spotted, rumpled hand, and I took it. It was warm, rough.

"I will."

"I think maybe you will." He let go, and I let his hand slip away reluctantly. "He may not, though." He pointed his chin at Enrique.

"Parents..." He shrugged. "Something to think about."

I thought about it all the way home.

I visited several times after that. I went to the outreach office on the Blemish, I talked to the team there, I read the propaganda. I brought Enrique, some of the time. Once, I even used their decrepit cosmetikit to wipe my mask, and sat unmade at an outside cafe for almost a quarter hour. Nothing happened. People came by, said hello, chatted about the weather, and went on their way. It was almost normal. After a while, I forgot to be self-conscious, and I got used to the marks, the bald spots, and, yes, the wrinkles. I couldn't deny that 'wrinkly' was an appropriate name, but it no longer called up horror or disgust. Instead, I thought of Jose and his fresh fruit juice, of the people who walked boldly and baldly through the streets of Wrinkletown just like regular people.

It came to a head one night, as I knew it had to. Probably I wanted it to. Certainly I was applying thinner and thinner masks at home in the evening, and going unmade during the day. One day, when I was finalizing some report structures for the desk to produce, Brendan came home early. He had take-out — a hot wedge of the Moldovan corn-cake I liked. I suppose it was a peace offering. He brought it into the study, calling out "Your order of *mamaliga*, sir."

I stood and turned, a big smile on my face. At last we were back on track.

I'd forgotten that I had no mask on. I don't know what Bren's face looked like beneath his. But it must have been bad; I could see a frown show through, and I heard him gag.

"Bren!" I cried, throwing my hands over my face. "Wait!" But he was already putting down the mamaliga, already turning down the hall to the nursery. I stood in his path, hands at my side, as he carried our unmade son back toward me. "Bren, stop." He refused to look at me, just pushing past with a face as smooth as china. "Bren, we can talk about this."

"There's nothing to talk about." His voice was raw as he stood at the door, his back to me. "You've gone too far, Jene. Think about Enrique." His voice broke, and I could see his arms trembling. Over his shoulder, our son made a happy face as he drooled on Brendan's coat. "I can't take, it Jene. I can't ... I can't come home to see a monster. To see you've made a monster of my son. You're going somewhere, Jene. I ... see that." His voice turned bitter. "I can't help seeing it. But I can't join you, Jene. Wherever you're going, go alone." He opened the door, and was gone.

I went looking for him, of course, the next day. I wore my Saja-designed mask and called our friends, visited his office. They wouldn't talk to me, wouldn't let me in. Eventually, I heard from Brendan's lawyer. We'd never had a lawyer before. She looked nice; probably client interface mask #3.

"Let me put it to you plainly, Jene."I could hear sympathy mixed with distaste. "The marriage is through." I'd figured that out already. I'd done my crying, and I'd come past begging. Especially since I knew what must be coming. "And so are your parental rights. Either you return your appearance to community standards, or you won't see Enrique again."

I closed my eyes. My mask was proof against tears, but I couldn't stand to see that smooth, friendly, false face, and know that mine was the same.

"You mean, put up a false front," I managed at last. "Give up my beliefs."

"Call it what you like. Those are the terms. Have your lawyer call me when you decide." She clicked off.

I didn't have a lawyer, of course. No one would take me. As soon as they heard my problem, they waved me off. "We don't do ... that," was the usual line, always delivered with calm, smiling, supportive face that showed nothing of what they felt and everything of who they were.

Saja was still talking to me, at least. "Just wear the masking," she said. "What difference does it make?" She was setting the latest trend — a shadow pattern that seemed hide her features in permanent shade.

"What difference? I don't know. The difference between truth and lies? Real and fake?"

The shadows moved across her face, her expression mysterious. "Happiness or no happiness? Are you happy, Jene?"

She knew I wasn't. No husband, no child, and, it turned out, not many friends. I had my principles to keep me warm at night, my work to keep me company during the day. Even the work seemed to be drying up as word got out.

"I shouldn't have to choose," I insisted, as if someone would care. "Enrique is my son as much as his. Why should I have to lie to keep him?"

She shrugged. We'd already had all the arguments about truth and beauty. "We all lie about something. Mostly to others. Sometimes to ourselves. It's all a question of pride. Do you have too much to love your son?"

That was the question that troubled my nights. Brendan was a lost cause. I knew that, even as it broke my heart. Enrique, though, still loved me. He was the only one who didn't care what I looked like. It would be silly to wear a mask in order to keep him. It would be wrong. But it would work, and the only person to pay would be me.

Truth or justice. That's what a lot of decisions come down to. We like to believe it's easy, but we know it's not. It never is. In the end, I called the only people I thought might know more about it.

"I had the same," said Jose, topping up my juice. "I had two daughters. They live with their mother, now. On their birthdays, I used to make up, go and see them. Now..." With no mask to swallow them, the tears rolled wet and dark down his crumpled face. "Here," he said, pulling framed photos from under the bar. "This is Linda. This one with the ribbons, that's Magi — Magdalena."

They were teens, made up in a style that had been popular some years back. I remembered the vivid jags of color, the oversized eyes. "And now?"

He shrugged, took the photos back in his hands. "I don't see them now. When they grew up, ... It was embarrassing for them. I was."

"So I should go back? Wear the mask?" I couldn't let Enrique slip away, couldn't end up alone like Jose.

"I don't know." He put the photos back under the bar, arranged them just right. "Things have changed. Maybe it's different now. Maybe not."

Give up my principles and keep access to my child? What would he think of that when he was older? What would I? Give up my child for the new self I'd only just found? What would he think of me now? In a few years, would he think of me at all?

Sometimes, when none of the choices work, you just have to make your own. If no one's on your side, make new sides. With advice from Jose and a few others who'd lost their kids, I chose to fight.

So that's my argument, Your Honor. Yes, I did those things. Yes, I moved to Wrinkletown. Yes, I go unmade. I'm not ashamed of it. This mask I have on? That's not my face; it's something my sister made up for me. It's not me. It's a fake, a fraud, a little piece of cosmetic trickery to make people think I'm perfect. I'm not. But I'm a good father. My son loves me. He doesn't care what I look like. I sound like Dad, I smell like Dad, I play like Dad. That's all he cares about. That's all that matters.

About the story

I've never been a fan of cosmetics. Most of them have historically been tested on animals, and most people I know look better as their natural self. Perhaps because I live in Oregon, most people I know don't wear makeup, but I know some that always do. I suppose I was pondering this when it occurred to me to write a story about a culture where people are never see others' true selves at all, and where it's taboo to do so.

I started with the idea that a makeup kit would be defective, and the person would be forced to be seen. I wasn't sure whether they would find or found a community of cosmetic-free people, but as the story developed, it became clear that such people were already around, just disregarded.

I did deliberately avoid specifying the protagonist's gender, because it didn't seem relevant to me. However, I was surprised by how many people found it hard to adapt their impressions to the final reveal that the narrator is a man.

Minstrel Boy Howling at the Moon

The red dirt of the plains was baked into his hands, making rivers of the creases in his palm, flowing off the low hills into the grasslands of his wrist. A summer of post-setting had left his hands as hard as brick and just as red.

"I'm gonna call you Gomda from now on," Matt at the Lov'n'Stop had said, sarcastically, "'cause you're gonna blow out of here like the wind."

He wouldn't leave, though. He'd been born in the dust of La Fave, and he'd likely die here, no more Native American than half of Oklahoma.

"What's *your* Caegu name?" he'd asked.

"Matt," his friend had answered. "But you can call me Adoette, 'cause I'm big like a tree."

"Big like a sapling, maybe." And that had been it for his make-believe Indian heritage—as fleeting as his chance of leaving town, or of ever being more than Deputy Assistant Manager at La Fave's only gas station and bus stop.

"Why *deputy* assistant?" he'd asked on his first day as Matt walked him through the pumps and the once-a-week bus schedule. "There're only two of us."

"You make a good point, Rafael," the Lov'n'Stop manager had admitted. "You don't look like a Rafael. Rafaels should be tall and graceful and angelic. I'm gonna call you Rafe. You okay with that?"

And because no one had ever given him a nickname, he'd nodded and said, "Sure. Rafe. Why not?"

"Tell you what, Rafe. Let's give you a trial run as deputy assistant. Maybe after six months or so, when you're handling the bus terminal all by yourself, we'll consider bumping you up to assistant manager."

"Or deputy manager," he'd said, and that was the moment they'd become friends.

Two years later, Rafe-Gomda was running the terminal by himself and had been for twenty-three and a half months, except for summer weekends building fences. The terminal consisted of a bench with two broken slats, under the eaves of the gas station, next to the electric cooler. Running it consisted of selling a ticket to Sally Guzman, who went to visit her sister in Boise City once a month for a week at a time.

"Me voy a Boise," she said, every time. "Hasta la vista, La Fave," which she pronounced Fah-veh.

"Tráenos unas papas," he'd say, although Boise City was in Oklahoma, not Idaho, and the potatoes there we no more famous than anywhere else. And what would he do with a bunch of potatoes, anyway?

He'd kept the deputy assistant manager title. After a week, it had been obvious that there was no future at the Lov'n'Stop, no more than there had been at the Pizza Hut, or at Bob's Tires and Hardware, or any of the places before that and after high school. But he'd stayed, selling one bus ticket a week, and pumping gas for Doris Gudic, who wanted to be treated like the prom queen she'd been twenty years back, and whom he occasionally slept with, when they were both bored.

"And when aren't you bored?" Matt asked as they sat out back of his trailer on a Tuesday night. Off to the left, the brick side wall of Gio's Pizza proclaimed "La Fave, OK" in proud, hand-sprayed letters. The official graffito of Oklahoma.

"There's gotta be more," Rafe said, his voice faltering as he recognized in himself the plaintive voice of every youth in every film and every novel. "More than this," he mumbled.

From around the corner, they could hear the rumble from Gio's Drive-In—an old projection TV set on a box; free entry with every pizza.

"Play something," Matt said, digging into the cooler for a new ice cube for his water. "Drown that shit out. Know how many times I've seen that movie? Never. Know how many times I've heard it?"

"Not in the mood." Rafe felt in his pocket for his harmonica. They sold them at the Lov'n'Stop. Or they had them, at least. The only one they'd "sold" had been to Rafe, and Matt had given it to him in lieu of a raise on his first anniversary.

"You get too bored, and Sende'll come round, play tricks on you. Spirits are like that."

"Sure. You ever wonder what it was like, back when the buffalo—"

"Roamed? Back before the white man came and killed them all?" Matt did his best to look self-righteous, but he wasn't good at it.

"Don't give me that shit. Indians killed 'em, too."

"Bison."

"What?" asked Rafe, feeling maybe they were on different conversational tracks after all.

"Bison, not buffalo. Buffalo are... different."

"I'm awed by your native wisdom."

"Whatever. Play something."

Rafe took the harp from his pocket. A wistful moan slid across the dry, caked soil of the lot and out into the low grass of the plains. A lament for the vanished buffalo, he decided. Bison. A quick arpeggio and they thundered into view, a hundred strong, a thousand. Slowing, they settled into a low, drawn-out arc of horns and shaggy coats. Close at hand, a mother chewed her cud while her calf nuzzled her belly.

He blew a couple of high notes and the calf stamped her feet, spreading her stance to get a better angle on her mother's udder. *You push in there. Live big while you can.* He tipped his head at the calf. *And you be good to her, Mama. Don't you leave her to go to the big city with your boyfriend.*

The mother rolled her eyes at him. She *saw* him. "I see you, too," he said, putting the harp down. The eternal verities acknowledged, she turned her back and faded into the night, leaving only grass and dust and the sound of helicopters from the drive-in.

"What's that?" Matt roused from where he'd leaned his chair against the trailer. "Must've dozed off. And what's that *smell*?"

"Bison," said Rafe, sliding his harp back into a pocket. "Buffalo."

"Let me guess. They vanished into a big mountain. That one, maybe." Matt pointed off toward Amarillo, or maybe the grain silo that was the highest point between there and here.

"Not even a little mountain. They just vanished away. Like a Snark."

"You and your Snark. Treat people with respect, I say. Now go home. It stinks out here, and I gotta get up at the same time as always tomorrow."

He'd played his buffalo song since then, but they hadn't come back. Not even the mother with her sarcastic eyes, or the calf with her hungry muzzle.

"Needs Sende's magic," Matt said.

"You wouldn't know magic if it bit you in the ass. Do the Caegu even have magic?"

"How the hell would I know? We got health care and we got a casino. If we had magic, do you think you'd be here? If we'd had magic, the white man would never have gotten past Arkansas."

"You know I'm not white, right? I mean, I'm right here in front of you."

"Whatever. White, Latino, Choctaw, all the same."

"Honorary Caegu, man. You can call me Gomda."

"Oh. Right. Bring on the magic, then." But he'd seemed oddly pensive as he said it.

It was a Sunday evening when the magic worked again. He'd given up on buffalo calling, and was making it up as he went along, sitting out at the edge of town in a jumble of rock Matt called the Bear Rocks, because not even sagebrush could get a purchase there. It was just the kind of joke he liked, and he'd made a point of explaining how 'Bare' should be spelled.

"More work than the joke is worth," Rafe had said, but he liked to come out here anyway, to sit under the overhang of a big rock and watch the setting sun cast shadows across the land.

He'd been playing for a while, trying to overbend a single reed without losing the melody, when he heard voices. Girls, it sounded like, but he kept on playing. There were no girls or even youngish women in town who'd be interested in him. Just Doris Gudic, and even she'd started going around with Hamel Norton, who ran the Arby's and preached on Sunday.

He thought he'd mastered the overbending trick, and the melody was just starting to get interesting when he heard the girls squealing. It sounded like fun at first, but then there was the noise of scrambling, and a panic to the voices, and he heard one screaming, "Bear!" though it wasn't quite "bear" that she said.

He threw down the harp and bolted up from beneath the rock, only to slam his head against the overhang. He dropped to his knees, stars dancing behind his eyes like roman candles in a nighttime sky. "Bear!" he heard again, and a growl like stone teeth grinding against each other.

Bear, he thought, fighting back to his feet. *No bear, no bison. No girls.* Not in La Fave, OK.

Out from under the rock, there were bears all right. Three of them, and they were tall, the height of the streetlights in Boise City. He shook his head, and it hurt enough to kill even the thought of dreams, but the bears were still there. They were growing, even, standing upright against a boulder that had thrust up from red dirt like the single tooth of a giant, left over from some fight amongst the ancients.

That wasn't there before. But it was here now, with three girls in dresses striped in green and yellow clinging to its peak. It grew taller as he watched, just barely outstripping the growth of the bears who clawed at it.

Well, shit, he thought, and found himself running, not wisely, toward the bears and their savage claws. As he ran, he saw the claws tear great chunks of the boulder loose and send them tumbling down like enormous hailstones.

He ran flat out, but the bears seemed as far away as ever. He realized they were shrinking, dwindling, waning with the sun, until, just as it dipped below the horizon, they were gone entirely, and he was alone.

Panting, hands on shaking knees, his head aching and wet with what must be blood, he turned back to the girls. They, too, were vanishing, the green and yellow stripes of their dresses fading away into the night and the stars, and the boulder they'd been standing on softened into the gray cloud of a thunderstorm. He was alone.

"I like the hat," Matt said on Monday when they opened the station. Rafe had done what he could using the bathroom mirror of his tiny apartment behind the post office, but he hadn't gotten the bandage to stick well, and it had come off in the night, leaving him a bedsheet caked with blood. He'd put a new bandage on this morning, but it wasn't any better.

He told Matt the story as they turned on the pumps and watched Hamel Norton fill up his big Dodge pickup.

"That's not cool," said Matt, making a note on Hamel's tab as Rafe wrapped up his story and the truck drove away. There was a bite to his voice Rafe had never heard before.

"No shit, it's not cool. I'm going crazy here."

"Uh-huh. And you just happened to go crazy after reading one of those *Kiowa Folktales* pamphlets, huh? Fuck you." He turned to the wire rack of pamphlets and postcards and sunglasses that only lost tourists ever bought from. "You're paying for that pamphlet, asshole." He riffled through the pamphlets in the rack. "You put it back, huh? You're paying for it just the same."

"What the hell, man? What are you talking about? I didn't touch your damned pamphlets."

"Sure you didn't." Matt turned back from the pamphlets with a look of bitter anger. "That's $3.50. Or I can take it out of your pay."

"What the ...? I didn't *take* it."

"Maybe you just borrowed it, along with some land. The tribes have heard that one before, *Gomda*."

It was another half-hour before they were talking to each other again, and another hour beyond that before Matt was calm enough to listen.

“Let me see that head,” he said at last. “Looks like one of your bears put that on for you.” He whistled when he saw the wound, and insisted on smearing antibiotic across it before taping down a new piece of gauze. “Need to cut your hair off when you get home, for that to stick right.” He pursed his lips. “It does look bad, though, I’ll give you that. Any more and you’d need to keep Sally company on her trip to Boise this afternoon.”

Rafe shuddered. He’d done that once, and she’d talked all the way about her family in Sinaloa, and how they must know his, even though his grandad had come from Sonora, and none of them had been back since. “It’s not that bad.” It hurt like hell.

“Well, I’m guessing you hit your head pretty hard. And probably you read one of these pamphlets at some point.”

Probably he had. He’d read pretty much everything there was to read in the station. And most of what there was in town.

“You’re saying I imagined it.” He didn’t believe it for a moment.

“Misremembered, Gomda.” But he said it without the bite this time. “No telling what something like that’ll do to you. ‘Blow to the head’ and all. It’s in all the cop shows.”

“There’s that tribal wisdom again.”

“No, seriously. I mean, that’s a Caegu folktale, alright. My dad told it to me, and his dad before him. Tso’ Ai, he called it. Bears’ Lodge. And the girls turn into stars. Seven of them.”

“What, like the Pleiades?”

“Yeah, them.”

“Well, I only saw three. Three girls, three bears.”

"You blaming me for your cut-rate, knock-off hallucination?"

"I guess not."

"So play me some bears, then."

"What, now?"

"We look busy to you?" There wouldn't be another rush until three or four cars came by at lunchtime.

"I haven't cleaned out my harp," Rafe said. It had been caked with red dust when he made his way back to it by moonlight, head aching and with a powerful urge to sleep. He'd felt lucky to make it home without passing out.

"What's a little dust going to do to it? Blow it out, anyway."

He'd played most of the rest of the day, but there'd been no bears, no girls, no growing stone teeth.

"Blow to the head," Matt said, and they left it at that.

He played frequently after that, overbending notes with ease now, but no bears appeared, and no bison.

"You be careful," Matt warned him. "Could be wolves next." He sounded more worried than joking.

"You ever heard of a wolf around here?"

"You ever heard of a bison?"

They left it at that, but Rafe still played whenever he got the chance.

"You're pretty good with that," Doris said. Her thing with Hamel hadn't worked out. "I could put in a word for you, maybe. I got a promoter friend who comes through Boise City once in a while. Maybe he knows a band needs a harmonica player." She seemed doubtful, as if the chances of anyone *needing* a harmonica player were slim to nothing.

"Could you?" He'd never thought about it before, never come up with a plan that could realistically get him out of La Fave. Probably this wouldn't either. Still ... "Do that for me. I'd be," he grinned and raised an eyebrow, "*mighty* grateful."

She giggled. "I'd like to see that." And they had gone on to other things.

It was a cold day in October, and he'd gone out to the Bear Rocks to practice. Doris had taken a tape off to meet her promoter friend—all the way to Amarillo, and, "Don't think you don't owe me." She'd be back tomorrow, but she'd called to say her friend said Rafe had "potential."

His mind was full of cities and billboards and marquees, of crowds and swank hotel rooms and high floors where you could see humanity spread out below you like a map of the future. He was blowing a soft, sad, bluesy kind of thing in a minor key, wondering whether he should try to remember it for later, and whether anyone would want to hear it. As he blew, the afternoon closed in like fog, until it felt almost like he was underground. He stood, careful of his head, still playing, and he could see the sun above him, and a clear sky. No bears. No bison looking down. But below ground.

The walls of the pit were steep, and his name was carved on each one. He blew harder, happier, but the walls remained. At last, he stopped. "Hey!" he called. "Not funny." Though the bears hadn't been funny, either.

Above, visible in the daytime sky, the moon winked back at him. Metaphorically. Magic could only do so much, apparently.

"Hey, moon," he called. "Joke's over."

The moon didn't answer, but there was a snuffling sound from the rim of the hole, and a head looked over.

Rafe closed his eyes. "Thanks, Matt," he muttered. A wolf. Of course it was wolves. Matt had promised wolves.

The snuffling multiplied, and more heads looked over—wolf heads with long muzzles, long tongues, and long teeth. And powerful paws that soon enough began digging at the edges of the pit, throwing red dirt aside with abandon.

Rafe looked around. There were no weapons in the pit; not even a stone. The hardest thing to hand was his six-inch harmonica. Not much of a weapon at the best of times, and little use against a hungry wolf.

So much for his debut in Amarillo. The wolves had a ways to go yet, but they would make it. At this rate, it would take less than an hour.

If he'd been religious, he might have prayed. Instead, he played his harp. No attempt at magic this time, no fancy phrasing. Just music from the heart, a swaying, fluid rhythm built on red dirt and tall grass and wind. Maybe some spirit would like it. Maybe not. It didn't matter. What mattered was that it was true, that whatever Rafe knew of life was in it—dull evenings in La Fave, evanescent bison at the edge of town, sagebrush, and rocks, and Doris Gudic, and two trips to Boise City.

The wolves had made a wide ramp down to shoulder level, and he leaned against the back wall and watched them dig. They'd started knocking the loose dirt into the pit now, and soon enough, one jumped down to stand on the pile. Its panting head was level with his, and he could smell the slightly foul taint of its breath. He closed his eyes, still playing, and heard its breathing as it reached its muzzle out and ... licked him.

He opened his eyes and it was still there, big head, big teeth. Big tongue, slapping him once on each cheek, and on the forehead. It bared its teeth in a wide smile. And then bounded back up to the ramp, and, in a wave of wolf tails, disappeared. Fading into the distance, he heard the pack howl a welcome.

He climbed the ramp before it could disappear as well, and found himself standing in the ordinary Oklahoma daylight. Behind him, the pit remained. It remained as he walked back to town, for as far as he could see.

It was still there the next day, when Matt came with him. There were wolf prints clear in the soft red dirt of the ramp, though they petered out as they headed away from the pit.

"Sende," Matt said. "That, or you gave me a blow to the head when I wasn't looking. Or we've both started drinking all of a sudden."

"Trickster god, right? Like Coyote?"

"Something like that. I guess. I don't know. I'm not really up on religion. Grandad used to talk about the sun. Pae. I don't know whether Sende's technically a god."

"Fair enough. I never got the whole Holy Trinity thing, myself."

A pit was a pit, and they exhausted its possibilities in under an hour.

"What'd Doris say?" Matt asked as they walked back to town and the overdue opening of the Lov'n'Stop. "Her friend, I mean."

"He's passing the tape on. He said he knows a guy could maybe get me some session work in Lubbock. Maybe Austin, even."

"Big time."

"Yup."

"'Course, the bus terminal keeps you pretty busy. Not like there won't be work if it doesn't pan out."

"Countin' on it. What would Sally do without me?"

"Probably get on the wrong bus, bring us back a sack of Idaho potatoes."

They walked on a ways in silence.

"I hope it works," Matt said as they turned down Main, where it became Route 325. "If you want it to."

"Me too," said Rafe after a while. "Me too." But he wondered whether a world of hotels, and crowds, and marquees would have any room for magic—whether there, beneath the city lights, he'd wish he were still back in La Fave, smelling bison and wolves, looking up at the moon and watching the stars wink back.

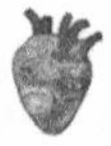

About the story

I'm a fan of the late singer-songwriter, Jimmy La Fave, and I lifted the title of my story directly from the title of one of his songs, from his *Highway Trance* album. La Fave sang what he called 'red dirt music', centered on Oklahoma, so I placed the story in an invented OK city, and built it in part on local mythology. Another of his songs, "Buffalo Return to the Plains" forced its way into the story without an invitation, but I let it stay.

Much to my delight, C.C. Finlay picked it up for *F&SF*, and it published in Sheree Renée Thomas' first issue as editor. *F&SF* has long been my dream market, and publishing there gave me the pleasant difficulty of having to find a new goal.

Fetch

She had died from overheating. It was an unlikely death, in the star-spark darkness beyond the atmosphere, where the outside temperature measured in single digits Kelvin. Yet temperature in space flight was a tricky thing. In Laika's case, a part of the ship had failed to separate. Torn insulation and a compromised control system had cooperated to simulate an intolerable summer day. She had died in hours.

His own cabin had multiple failsafes, multiple mechanisms to compensate for radiative heat loss, for the lack of convection, advection, conduction. And of course they watched him. Just like they'd monitored Laika, but with cameras.

He faced his favorite now, the smooth curve of glass like HAL's dark and ominous eye, but with only human intelligence behind it. "Hello," he said. It would take a year for the message to reach Earth. There was no hurry. Not anymore.

'Leica', read the white lettering curved above the purple of the lens. He'd pasted a softscreen up beside it, with a color image of Laika in her cramped training cage. She'd been unable to turn around. She'd stopped urinating.

"No need to worry, girl." After a while, he'd gotten used to the limited movement, the claustrophobia. Drugs had helped. He had his four by four by four — sixty-four glorious meters of freedom in an ungainly cube. The clumsy bulk of it didn't matter. The cube was empty of everything but air, which might as well be stored here as in the outside tanks.

He was small, of course. On the growth front, Asian and Latin genes had won out against European and Scandinavian, producing a short, blond, tan-skinned man with blue eyes. Like Laika's he liked to think; the records weren't clear, but she'd been part Husky. The New Frontiers project had loved him from the start. He could have been dreamed up in a public relations brainstorm for the brand-new United League of Earth and its shiny, attention-distracting launch to the edges of the solar system. A Swedish grandmother for robust health, a Venezuelan Wayuu one for compact durability, cancer-free grandfathers who'd survived Chernobyl and Fukushima for radiation resistance. American parents working in foreign aid who'd brought him up in Guinea, Liberia, Rwanda, Tanzania — always heading east in search of something they'd never found.

"Well, *we've* found something, haven't we, Laika?" He'd made history, in any case. Furthest man in space. First human to the Oort cloud. First to stake a claim on behalf of the United League. Even after fifty years in transit, no one had gotten here first, no one had zipped past with new technology and a shrug of apology. Earth would send congratulations, no doubt. They might even have thought to send them in advance. Despite the morning's diagnosis. Or perhaps because of it.

He'd proved it was possible, proved that with drugs and smarts and entertainment, it was possible to stay sane.

"Mostly," he acknowledged to Laika. "Mostly sane." There had been a few dark periods. Every life had those. "You helped." He reached out to stroke the screen, and she arched her neck to one side. The animation had been tricky. It had taken months to get close, years to perfect. Earth hadn't helped. Hadn't known to help, though they would have been willing.

"Cutaneous radiation injury, they said," he told Laika, though she'd heard it already. "Plus, maybe," he checked the morning's message, "leukopenia, thrombocytopenia, erythema, keratosis, and telangiectasia. But you knew that, didn't you, girl?" He'd run out of clean cloth for bandages. There wasn't enough water left to wash them effectively. He could soak them, but then the cycler took time to process the murky fluid. He'd tried boiling the ooze off the bandages in the airlock, but of course it made the water shortage worse. And then the bandages were cold. He settled for changing bandages every hour, letting the damp ones dry in the cabin until the room was oppressively dank and smelly.

"Sorry, girl," he shrugged at Laika. "Scrubber can't keep up." Only the sail controls and radio worked well these days. "Software error." He coughed, a spray of straw-pale fluid that floated across the cabin like a cloud. "Problem in the flesh drive." Laika cocked her head and wagged her tail to laugh.

Would he have lived longer on Earth? It seemed unlikely. Less radiation, of course. If he'd avoided Luanda, Bishkek, Winnipeg, and the other places the UL had pacified. Had there been more, after he left? It didn't matter. New Frontiers had taken him on, more sold on his heritage than on hard-won but second-rate degrees in astronomy and medicine, but they'd taken him. He owed them for that, anyway.

And for Mor-Mor. After the terror attacks, she'd been the only family he had left. A bedridden old Swedish woman in a flat in a suburb of Vänersborg, itself now a suburb of Trollhättan. She'd lived only for weekly visits from the therapy dogs, and video-chats from one lone grandson, when he could afford them.

"She didn't have you though, did she, girl?" Laika wagged and barked. "That's the spirit." Mor-Mor had believed firmly in spirits — and ley-lines and charms and all the things her Methodist parents had disapproved of. 'Your parents' spirits are somewhere in the world,' she'd told him. 'It's just up to you to find them.' But when his search had taken him off Earth, she hadn't fought it.

'I need to go,' he'd told her. And, because he wanted to do it, really wanted to, and because he had nothing else, she'd let him go. 'Take this,' was the only thing she'd said, and sent a scan of Laika, faded black and white from some old newspaper, stained with the tears she'd wept back in the 20th century, and in the years since. 'I want to go,' he'd assured her, though she already knew. 'I choose to go.'

He wouldn't trade it for anything, half a century on. He'd accomplished little beyond a study in isolation, little that an automated probe could not have done better. He'd read up on the law, during his voyage, confirmed that the trip was more symbolic than precedential, and let it go. He'd read thousands of books, written a handful of his own.

"I had to go," he told Laika now. The pay for his effort had settled Mor-Mor in an elegant home with a view of the dog park, bought her the best care that he'd never told her was his real reason for going. The rest had funded a small dog rescue foundation. Would he have accomplished more had he stayed, worked his way out of poverty and into the middle class like a few lucky others? In her last message, some forty years back, now, she'd told him he was right to go. It was hard to tell, through the UL censors, but he'd taken it as a confirmation that things had gotten worse. He'd sent her back a still from his Laika simulator, then capable of little more than an exaggerated doggy grin.

"But you can do more than that now, can't you girl?" She wriggled and rolled over in her little space. It took some maneuvering. "Of course you can."

He'd done some wriggling himself, over the years. When even the drugs weren't enough to calm him, when he needed motion, he had the Track — a circular tube running around the outside of his cube. A meter wide; just enough to pull himself along in endless circles, or to pump his legs a bit on the clever ratchet-cycle New Frontiers had built.

There was more room now, of course. On two ends of the cube, a hatch led to empty tanks and holds. If he wanted, he could pressurize them, wander past their complex struts and bulkheads like a spelunker exploring lost caverns.

"After a while, the space doesn't matter," he told Laika. "Your perspective shifts." All that food and water had provided shielding. Laika had had none, but she hadn't lived long enough for it to matter. Here, the cycler reused everything it could. Over a fifty-year journey, though, there were losses. The holds were bare now. Over the years, they'd held spares, gardens, waste, play areas, meditation chambers. There had been years when he lived in them, heedless of exposure. Years when he'd hidden in his little cube core. Now it made no difference. He checked his bandages, an old jumpsuit torn in strips. The seepage wasn't bad. Not troubling.

"Is it time?" he asked Laika. She quirked her head to one side, ears cocked. "Do you think it's finally time?" She quirked her head the other way, eyes eager, tongue lolling just to the edge of her teeth. "It's now or never, girl." They'd given him a year to live, the UL doctors, in the message they'd sent a year ago. "Shall we do it?"

"Arf!" she replied, with a naughty gleam in her eye.

"I thought so too," he agreed. And of course he'd been planning this for years. Ever since Mor-Mor died, in a way.

"I'm turning the sail," he announced to his distant audience. They still listened, still watched. He got weekly messages, advice on problems no longer relevant, suggestions for synthesizing drugs from materials long out of inventory, advice on how to compact waste he'd long since dumped. "I'll be out of touch for a while." It was a dereliction of duty, his first in fifty conscientious years. Without the sail to focus their faint signals, he would no longer hear Earth's messages, no longer be able to send his own.

"We did our part, though, didn't we, girl?" Laika grinned back. "I think we did." With a twinge of guilt and uncertainty, ruthlessly suppressed, he tapped the icon for his pre-calculated sail shift. It would take weeks.

He set the second program running. He'd recorded his message over months, short as it was. "I wanted to get it just right," he told Laika and the lens that no longer transmitted his image and voice. In the circuits behind the control panel, gates opened and closed, feeding a short, recorded message to the radio in a cycle of thousands of slightly different iterations. "It was mostly programming and calculation, actually." He scratched her head, and she bowed her neck in pleasure. Her tail thumped against her cage, only the tip visible beyond the curve of its metal roof.

"I'll just check the readouts," he said, withdrawing his hand.

"Arf!" she said, asking for more scratching. When none came, she lay her head down between her paws and settled into her resting state. This far from the Sun, energy was scarce. The micro-reactor worked only at a low level, and battery capacity had dwindled with time.

The sailcord readouts were tied to the main screen, of course, but he liked to climb out and check the physical gauges when he could. He still had a working pressure suit, and of course exposure didn't matter anymore. He tied another layer of cloth around his weeping chest. Body fluids loose in the suit could get in the circuits if they really tried. More important, they smelled bad. He smelled bad enough already. He felt bad for Laika, with her more sensitive nose. Of course, she was just a simulation.

Out on the hull, the sail was responding just as his simulation had predicted. It was early to say much, of course. The frozen bearings on #27 and the broken tension-pulley on #41 had required a little workaround, but it seemed to work just as it should.

He floated for a while sun-side. It didn't matter anymore if he drifted a bit. In the early days, the focus of the sail had been a dangerous place to be; it would have burned through his suit in seconds. Now it was barely warm.

Thousands of AUs away, Sol was a small, bright dot. "Bye," he said, and waved, as if he hadn't said his farewells years before. The motion set him slowly spinning. The view didn't change much. At this distance, even Sol didn't look like much. He watched as the Milky Way slowly circled around him until the tension in his twisting safe-line stopped him and set him spinning back the other way. "Hi."

They'd tried to stop him, of course, the do-gooders and the Luddites and the religionists. 'It's not fair,' they'd said, and 'You'll draw the attention of aliens,' and 'Man was meant to live on Earth.' But he'd had no family aside from Mor-Mor, he'd been young and handsome, and he'd had the League behind him, and the scientists, and the fear that the Confederation might get there first.

"Looks like we're out here alone," he told Laika. "No aliens. No angels. Darn." He tugged the safeline to set him moving slowly back to the ship. "And this way, I got to be with you." Mor-Mor had cried the day he left. 'Go find her,' she'd said. "And I will," he said now. "I know you're out here somewhere, kid." Because where else could the soul of a spacedog go? "Playing with those aliens, probably, eh?"

Somewhere in the ship, an algorithm parsed the statement, generated a response. "Arf!"

Back inside the ship, he listened to the messages that still accumulated despite the slowly-turning sail. Long-winded bureaucrats celebrating last year's 49th anniversary. Curt doctors detailing treatments he'd long since tried. Dull chemists proposing supplements scraped from hull surfaces and worn out suit parts.

He listened to it all. "Never know, eh, girl? Might be something good in there." After a few days, the sail had shifted enough that the messages were too broken for the computer to reconstruct. "Now we're really alone, hmm?" He checked the telltales. His message continued to go out in different codings, on different frequencies, as the sail slowly turned.

He slept for a time, woke with a start. "Thought I heard you barking." He stroked her neck. "Not you, hmm?" She reached out a paw for more scratching, and he rubbed a hand on each side of her neck, setting her wriggling like a puppy in her restraints. "Not yet. Not long."

He had no energy now to eat, and the water from the cycler was cloudy. "Smells bad, too. Well," he coughed, and droplets of red floated up to dot the camera lens. "You did without water. Guess I can too." He turned the speakers on so that he could hear his message, still transmitting, still repeating.

He settled his head comfortably against a cushion on the bulkhead, and listened to Laika breathing softly in his ear. Her muzzle came down soft against his shoulder and he smiled. "Good night, girl," he murmured. As his eyes grew dull, she settled into rest mode.

In the still of the cabin, a recording played on. A whistle, high, then low. Then an enthusiastic call, "Лайка, вернись домой. Тебе пора отдыхать." *Laika, come home. It's time to rest.* At the outer hatch, a scratching sound might have been the scrabbling of claws, asking to come in.

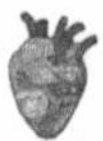

About the story

In 1957, the USSR sent a dog on the second craft ever to enter Earth orbit, Sputnik 2. The ship was never intended to be recovered, but Laika, a part-Husky street dog, died within hours of takeoff. When Adilya Kotovskaya settled Laika into her cramped space on Sputnik, she said "Please forgive us." Oleg Gazenko, who chose and trained Laika, later said, "The more time passes, the more I'm sorry about it. We shouldn't have done it. We did not learn enough from the mission to justify the death of the dog."

We've done a lot of terrible things to animals in the name of science (and continue to do them). The cruelty of Laika's death has haunted me since I was a child. My favorite film is Lasse Hallstrom's *My Life as a Dog*, in which a boy ponders what was done to Laika. This particular story, though, was inspired by a song from Tony Carey's Planet P Project, "Saw a Satellite", which includes the lines, "And the ratings went over the moon on the day Laika died / But my mother just stayed in her room all morning and she cried". I wanted to write something that both recognized the evil we did to Laika, but had a more hopeful, optimistic tone. I'm not sure it worked on the optimism front, but despite its grim inception, the story is intended as a positive message about coming to terms with the errors of the past.

The Humblebract Expedition

"He needs to have fun." The guildmaster put his hand lovingly on the back of a pudgy adolescent boy about my age. "I want him to have fun."

"He's right here," I answered tartly. Rich, the Iron Master might be, but I didn't appreciate being rousted from my bed at this time of morning. My mother, never greatly interested, had barely notice my going. "What does *he* want?"

The boy rolled his eyes, and I gave him a little more credit. Still, his father talked over him.

"I apologize, young lady, for the way you were brought here." He eyed his men, and I could see how this would go. "It's my fault." The family was just full of surprises. "I told them it was urgent." He paused, eyeing my rough canvas tunic against the rich brocade of his parlor chair. Weighing up what it would cost to buy me, I'd have thought, but I'd been wrong twice about him and his son already.

The boy surprised me once more, laying a gentle hand on his father's arm, at which the man immediately stilled and turned toward him.

"It's this way, Miss Tandarakel—" the boy said.

"Tando," I interrupted out of habit.

"Tando, then. I'm dying." It was subtle, but I could see how the father tensed, how his eyes tightened at the corners. He loved this boy for real. "I have the shiver sickness." The boy paused. "So do you." I nodded. No big secret there, not in Thicktown where I lived. "My father wants me to die happy. We think you can help."

This wasn't at all how I thought the meeting would go. The merchant class doesn't have a lot of time for those of us in Thicktown, except when they need miners or serfs or bearers or, in the case of the Iron Guild, strikers and bellows workers. I'd expected – and I was sure my mother had expected – an offer to buy me as a maid. I'd expected to tell them I had the shivers, and to go back home to bed. No point in buying a maid with only a few months left in her.

"Why me?" I was genuinely curious. "What do I know about ...," I waved a hand at the glossy wooden tables, the paneled walls, the fine curtains, "all this?"

The boy opened his mouth, but I could see the tremble in his jaw, and a quick blink of the father's wet eyes showed that he saw it too. I guessed that the boy was about month farther along in the shivers than I was. "You know about fun," the father intervened. "That's what they say, down in the Thick."

That was how it started. One day, making up stories for my friends to act out, down in the Thick while I waited to die; next day, paid playmate for Elda, shiver-stricken son of the city's Iron Master, Darlinantro k'Halsne.

"I meant what I said," the Master said, the next morning, in his rich parlor. Without his son there, he was all business – the sharp, calculating mind that had seen him win control of the forges and the iron mines. "I want Elda to have fun. He thinks you can do it. I'll pay you to make it happen." He eyed me coldly. "Enough to give your mother a home she owns. Enough to see her die comfortable." It wouldn't be long, his look said. Not in the Deep Thick where we live, where the roof was an old canvas sail we shared with a neighbor, and the rats knew how to knock the lid off the grain jar.

"She's happy where she is," I said. Obviously she wasn't. Who could be? But the first thing I'd learned in the Thick was to distrust anything that sounded good. Especially a first offer.

He scoffed. "You've moved three times in the last fourteen months. Twice for failure to pay rent, once because of your sickness. Even though it's not contagious." A trace of anger came through the smooth facade. "Your mother gets a little work from the bar down the alley, but it's been less and less since they heard about you." His lips tightened. "No one wants to take a chance."

I kept my eyes from widening. He know more about us than I had expected. Still, *never take the first offer*. "We'll work it out."

His eyes measure me. "I think you would. But this way you won't have to. You'll live here. I'll buy your mother a home on Alder street," this time my eyes did widen, "mm-hmm. And two gold pieces right now, one a month until ..."

"He dies," I said, thinking to help.

"Or you do," he agreed coldly. "That's the offer. Take it or go." *I may be hurting,* his voice said, *but I'm no fool, even for my son.*

I took it. I went personally to see the house on Alder, halfway through the Thick to the commercial sector where the tradesmen worked. It was small, clean, sound, with a thatched roof and a tiny little garden plot where the sun could just sneak past the Clothiers' warehouse to the south. I almost cried, when I showed the deed to a scribe and she verified that it said what it should. My mother did cry, and she fell to her knees when I gave her two golds, soft as they should be, and held in a little white sack. She could live on that for the rest of her life, if she were careful.

I knew she wouldn't be, but it wasn't my problem now. I'd cared for her, as I'd promised my father I would. What she did with herself now was her own issue.

The actual job, of course, was a little less clear. "He should have fun," the Master said. "He should ... die happy."

"Isn't he happy now?" I asked. Elda himself was upstairs in bed. He seemed to spend much of his time there. More than he should, if I'd gauged his sickness correctly.

The Master shrugged. "I think so. But I want him to *enjoy* himself. At least once." His voice trembled, but he got it under control. "That's your job."

I went up to see Elda, on the second floor of the Master's house, there high on the hill overlooking forests and meadows. He had a fine view from his huge bed. I sat on the edge of it, more to establish some parameters than because I wanted to. It was soft. Elda's eyebrow quirked, as if he knew exactly what I was thinking.

"So," he said.

"So," I agreed. We sat there for a while, looking out the window together. "What do you like to do?" I asked at last. It was as good a place to start as any.

"Read," he said with a shrug that said he knew I couldn't. "I like adventures," he added more helpfully. "Excitement. Heroes and monsters. The forces of Good winning out."

We shared a small smile that acknowledged we were both Good incarnate, and that neither of us was likely to win out.

"Right," I said. "Just need to find a monster, then." One that we could beat. I considered that for a while, looking at his pudgy form under mounds of cotton blankets. He'd been forthright so far, and I thought I owed him the same. "How long?"

"Have I got?" He was quick, alright. "Two months. Two and a half, perhaps. You?"

"Four," I told him. "Better get started on that monster, then."

He laughed. "You tell stories, they say. Tell me one now, while I dress."

I told him the one about Dernkhina and the glass sword that she could never use, and he cheered in the all the right places, stopping to act out her fatal blow against the Water Spider with just one leg in his breeches.

"You've got a flair for it," I said while he finished dressing.

"Weapons training," he said, leading me down the hall to the room next door. "Before. This is your room."

It was just like his, even down to a selection of clothes in roughly my size. A few dresses, but mostly stout boots and thick breeches and blouses. Perfect for adventuring. I changed quickly, marveling at how soft the cloth felt, and how odd it was not to feel the cool spot under my left arm, where the hole in my tunic had grown too large to darn.

We spent the next two weeks wandering through the parts of the city I'd never seen before - past mansions and townhouses, and even up to the edge of the Keep itself. It was fascinating, and I think we both had fun, exploring and daring each other to enter this store or another. The pair of bulky guards that trailed us were awkward at first, but we worked them into our travels soon enough. Their names were Raken and Telad, but Elda called them Smiley and Dwarf in his ironic way. I learned soon enough that he took little seriously, but also that a keen intelligence tired quickly of repetition.

Soon enough, we'd seen much of what the High Town had to offer. It was pretty, but not well suited to children running and playing, especially with guards running after, hands holding weapons to their sides. Instead, I proposed, we should head to the Thick.

"I don't like it," said Smiley with her characteristic frown.

"It'll be fine," I said, though while I was confident of Elda, I was less sure how my old neighbourhood would react to an armed merchant's man.

"Follow," said the tall, laconic Dwarf. By which he meant they'd been directed to follow us, not tell us what to do. I pressed the point, and soon enough, we were off down to the thick.

We played down there for the afternoon, with me as the Hermit and Elda the Naiad, running from the Ogres – played willy nilly by Smiley and Dwarf. Soon enough, we'd attracted attention – from my old friends, and from an older, harder crew with an ugly note to their muttering.

"Shiver...," I heard, and "guards," and "reward."

"Psst." My friend Corak was leaning out from behind a barrel, his gangly form half-shadowed. "You've got to go, Tand. The Fild Bar crew is getting ideas." Message delivered, he moved on to pleasantries. "What're you doing here, anyway? What happened? We heard your mother got signed on as a mistress or something. Is this him?" directed at Elda. "You worth a gold?" He seemed more curious than anything.

Smiley came up as well. "Clear off, boy," she said to Corak. To Elda, she said, "Sir, I think it best we leave. There's a bit of a crowd..." It was obvious now that the mood on the street had darkened, and any minute now an implicit threat would become overt.

"Must we?" asked Elda. He could see the crowd as well as we, but he was probably the only without the experience to read its meaning.

I took a second glance. I could see hands in pockets and behind backs, and the alleys closing one by one. "We must," I said, and exchanged glances with Smiley and Dwarf.

"Okay," said Elda, unseeing, but I could see the shiver starting in his hands. "But I may need a break."

"No time," I said, and scooted under his left arm. "Corak!" I said, and jerked my head. He followed my lead and took the other arm. "Alas, the Dragonet's fire had burned him sorely," I called, "and the hero's brave companions bore him away to safety." A little on the nose, but I was too worried to be creative. "Past the market," I hissed to Corak, and we dragged Elda off between us toward the stalls just visible at the end of the alley.

A quick glance behind showed that the guards had gotten the message, though Smiley was a bit of a ham. With a theatrical sigh, she shoved Dwarf in our direction, and, hand on dirk, followed reluctantly after us. I could see her shoulders tense, but we'd acted soon enough. A few moments and two streets later, the danger was past.

The excitement, though, had just begun.

"You took him to the Thick," the Master said. His voice was flat, calm, and deadlier than a Dragonet had ever been.

I shrugged, trying to play it cool. My own shivers sometimes emerged under stress, and I was fighting to stay calm. "You wanted him to have fun."

"You think kidnapping," he enunciated the word carefully and slowly, "would have been fun."

I thought of the crew that usually hung out at the Fild Bar – a decrepit hovel with two jugs of cheap vodka – and grimaced. "He has guards." I sounded sullen, even to myself.

"Listen to me." I got the feeling that he'd have liked to grab me by the collar of my new blouse if he hadn't been so controlled. "Listen very carefully. I want my son to die *happy*. And of *natural* causes." Though rumor was the shivers was a curse resurfaced from the old Mage Wars. "If he doesn't..." I think he wanted me to think I wouldn't either. Or my mother wouldn't. Or something. It wasn't much of a threat, though, because, first, I didn't really care, and second, because I didn't believe he'd do it. He might be as savage in trade as they said, but he wasn't vengeful. I could tell that from how he treated his son. "You're only here now, because ..."

And then I had it, and I could feel the incipient shivers drain away from me. "He had fun, didn't he? He had *fun!*" While Corak and I had been sweating with fear and exertion, and the guards had been waiting for that first rock or dagger in the back, Elda had been stumbling along, sick with the shivers, and having the time of his life.

"He did," the Master confirmed, with a harsh smile. "But you and I know better."

And I did, I realized. I'd lived in the Thick my whole life. Sure, I'd never been near the merchant class before, but I should have known better. I'd been stupid – too caught up in pride at my storytelling ability to think it through carefully. I nodded.

"Never again," the Master said, and it was a command, not a negotiation. I nodded again. "He trusts you," the Master said, a little puzzled. "But he's innocent. From now on, Raken takes the lead in any issue of safety. You will obey her." Again the command. Again, I nodded. "She spoke for you too. And your friend Corak," he added. "She even smiled." The corners of his eyes crinkled, and I wondered whether he might be close to smiling himself.

Elda was, if anything, even more excited when I saw him next. He'd added Corak to his retinue, somehow, and Corak had been telling him exaggerated stories of the villainy of the Fild Bar gang – it had grown in the telling from an irregular crew of drunkards and layabouts to an organized gang of bandits – and their cruel ways. Elda's eyes grew rounder and rounder, until I took Corak off for some bread and fruit to break our fast.

"He hired me on," Corak said as I led him down the hall. "The Master, I mean. Keep the youngster safe," he said, though Elda was his own age. "Kind of a bodyguard," he said stoutly.

Or nursemaid, I thought. *For when the shivers come again.*

"I'm glad," I said. And I was, I realized. Corak was solid, reliable, and he'd neither tried to grope me nor avoided me when the shivers came on me. He was a good addition.

"Need stay out of the Thick," Corak said as we came back up the stairs again, laden with a plate of bread and mouth-watering fresh fruit, and a pitcher water so clear you could see straight through it to the pewter bottom.

"Agreed." But what would we do instead? After true danger, even unrecognized, Elda would hardly be content to run around the house's garden playing elves and goblins. I'd need more. And I had a thought as to where to find it.

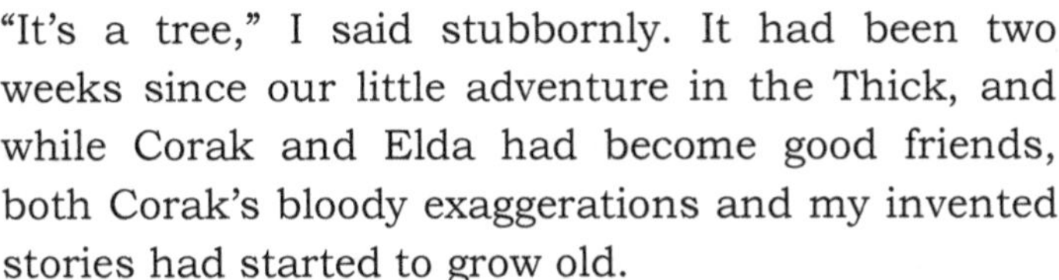

"It's a tree," I said stubbornly. It had been two weeks since our little adventure in the Thick, and while Corak and Elda had become good friends, both Corak's bloody exaggerations and my invented stories had started to grow old.

"A moving tree." The Master had insisted on pre-approving any excursions outside the immediate neighbourhood. "That eats things." Smiley, who had been required to join us, frowned even more than usual.

"No, sir." On this point I was firm. "That's the amblebract. It only grows in the Eastern Reaches, where the Mage War was at its... most active."

"Most destructive," said Smiley, who, like all of us, was generations too old to have any first-hand knowledge.

"A tree that moves, and captures animals and plants seeds in their corpses," insisted the Master coldly. "I thought you smarter, girl."

"That's the amblebract," I repeated. "But the Orchard master has made a cross of the amblebract and the humectin. That's a—"

"I know what a humectin is," he said. Which was more than I did. I'd heard it was like a melon and a plum, the size of my thumb, with tart green flesh and tiny seeds that stuck in your teeth. None of that meant much to me. Even in the Master's house, the fruit consisted mostly of apples and grapes.

"So, this cross, the ..." the name escaped me.

"Humblebract," offered Smiley, who had a dry sense of humor when you dug down to it.

"Sure," I agreed, though I was fairly sure the name had been longer and more formal. "Anyhow, the ... humblebract, isn't dangerous at all. What it does, is, it grabs you, and stuffs a fruit in your mouth.. That's it. Then it lets you go. Totally safe." There were a few caveats, as I understood it, but that was the gist.

"And you know that from...?"

"A friend," I said, not entirely accurately. I'd heard about it on the streets a few months back from Darithar – a somewhat cruel older boy who'd gotten a job in the orchards and liked to brag about it to the rest of us.

"And how that will be fun?" he asked. "You can shove fruit in each other's mouths here at home." For all I knew, Corak and Elda were doing that now. Their play tended to devolve into a wrestling that I didn't much care for.

"Well, Elda won't know." That, I'd decided, was the key to Elda's fun – a lack of appreciation of risk. Last time, he'd missed a risk the rest of us saw. This time, I was aiming for the opposite. "He'll find it scary. But he'll be safe the whole time," I insisted.

The Master pondered. "Very well," he said at last, just when I'd given up hope. "I'll talk to the Orchard Master. But first," he turned his hard gaze on me, "we will try it ourselves, you and I." He seemed to remember that Smiley was there, and amended, "The three of us."

And so, two days later, leaving Corak and Elda to their own devices, the three of us trooped off to the orchards outside the city – me, the silent Iron

Master, a grumpy Smiley, and a bevy of the Master's own guards.

The Orchard Master met us himself. "As a courtesy," he pointed out, "to another Master." He left it to a journeyman to explain the trees, however.

"...so it's a hybrid," she said. "Not just a splice or graft, but a true hybrid, developed from ten generations of careful cross-breeding. Luckily, it breeds quickly, the—"

"Humblebract," I said, nudging Smiley.

The journeyman looked up. "That's a good name, actually. You're a clever young girl." I could feel Smiley's eye roll matching my own. "Anyhow, we have a little grove of the fourth generation here now, in a little circle. It's a circle, because ..." The rest was very technical and had something to do with soils and senescence and other words I knew little about, and I spent the time eyeing the grove and thinking how to build a game around it.

"So it's quite safe," the journeyman finished, "so long as you remember these basic precautions." She was hold out what looked like a clothespin and a ball of wax. I took them reflexively.

I looked around. To my side, Smiley was splitting the wax in two large balls, and pushing them into her ears. To the other, the grim Master was carefully placing the wooden clothespin on his nose. I quickly followed suit, wishing I'd listened more to either the journeyman or my acquaintance Darithar and his caveats.

The journeyman, her own nose and ears already covered, said something, and tugged at her trousers in emphasis. They fit tightly at the waist, and I envied her her shapely hips. Mine had just barely begun to widen, and never would improve much. Still, my breeches fit close enough. She surveyed us all, nodded, and led us toward some trees.

They looked like willows – all dangly withes with bulbous tips, and shiny golden bark like nothing I'd ever seen, though my experience of trees was limited. As the journeyman approached, the withes twitched, and slowly coiled, up and around her until she was entirely encircled. They wrapped around her head, and I could see her mouth was open. A withe found its way inside, and with a little jerk, popped back. The little bulb at the end was gone, and I could see the journeyman's jaw working as the coils slowly released her.

She nodded to us, and we moved slowly forward. It had been my plan, but I was more reluctant than I'd anticipated. All that coiling and wrapping looked a lot more frightening than I had anticipated. Still, I could see the Master and Smiley moving in on either side, and I hurried to match them.

The withes were slower than I'd expected, but firmer, and as I moved on toward the tree, their pull became ever stronger, more inexorable, until I found myself with only one foot on the ground, unable to move. I could feel the withes moving around me, poking into pockets, snaking down the neck of my blouse, reaching up my breeches to the knee. They tried my neck, my head, my face. I was glad of the wax, and hoping the clothespin would hold on my nose when I finally recalled the way the thing worked. I opened my mouth, and let a bulb-ended withe find its way in. It coiled around in my mouth, and, apparently satisfied with conditions, let loose of the bulb with a pop that bounced it off the roof of my mouth. Reflexively, I bit down.

This was no grape. It had a delicate, subtle flavor at first, juicy, but with firm little nodes that I hoped were just the seeds. After time, the initial slight sweetness faded, leaving behind a tart taste a little like a sour apple, but not so drying. I bit down on one of the seeds, and it let out a tiny burst that reminded me of the smell of the almonds they sold hot in the market at WinterFeast. It was delicious.

When I opened my eyes again, the coils had fallen away, and the journeyman was urging me toward her, back away from the tree.

"... react again within a minute," she was saying when I dug the wax out of my ears, "so it's important to keep moving, whether in or out." She held her hand out, and I handed back the wax and, belatedly, the clothespin.

"Would they really...?" Smiley asked, handing back her own armor.

"Put a fruit in your nose? Absolutely. Or your ears, or anywhere else they find an opening. Tight pants, very important. Not really harmful, of course, but uncomfortable, getting those seeds out of your ... ears."

Even Smiley smiled at that.

The humblebract expedition was a huge success. I'd built it into a heroic story, where we had to cross through the grove to recover a stone of power from the Mage War, if only we could overcome its arboreal defenders, still doing their thing centuries later. Most, of course, succumbed to their seductive voices or poisonous vapors. And if we were trapped, as we likely would be, the only course would be to pretend to accept the treacherous seed of the trees and escape while they were distracted, to try again another day.

Elda knew, of course, that little of this was true – he'd had his own chat with his father after the Thick, of the 'more in sorrow than anger' variety – but he played along with enthusiasm. Corak, in his clumsy way, did his best to follow, though he knew the truth. As Elda's shivers had progressed, Corak had become nursemaid in truth, helping Elda to dress, to bathe, even to eat. I could see what I had to look forward to, and my own shivers had become more pronounced and frequent, though not so much as trouble me yet.

On the day of the expedition, we arrived to find we'd been handed off from the journeyman to, not even an apprentice, but a lowly laborer – my old acquaintance Darathar. He seemed sour to have been handed the duty, and even more so when he saw who arrived. If the journeyman had thought to unite similar types, she'd miscalculated.

"Know why you're here, do you?" Darathar's tone was sullen, and his canvas trousers, held up with rope, well worn along the seam, and with the pocket torn out, reminded me just how lucky I was to have left the Thick. His gaze suggested he'd had the same thought.

"All was explained," I said, holding up a hand, and trying to preserve the mystery as Darathar resentfully handed out wax and clothespins. "Let us now to to our places go, brave hearts," I said to get everyone moving beyond his voice. "Watch for my signal. And recall, there is no shame in leaving the battle to the future, if so we must."

My little team of Elda, Corak close beside, with Smiley and Dwarf to either side, fanned out. I headed the other direction so that they could see me across the grove, with Darathar a grumpy presence between us. He joined us in the grove, though.

"And I was the only one who made it all the way through to the center, Father," Elda said that night at dinner. His shivers had become more and more frequent, but he'd had a good morning, and in fact made it past his tree, which had concentrated on Corak. "But then I saw poor Corak trapped, and went back." That was true too; he'd gone back without hesitation, the only one of us who'd thought he was in real danger. "But then I got the shivers, and Corak had to rescue *me*, and we were lucky to escape with our lives." He knew better, by now, of course, but he looked up at Corak so warmly that the poor boy blushed. "That poor Darathar, though..."

We all smothered smiles. It wasn't really funny, of course, what had happened to him, with his loose, torn trousers, but he'd been so unpleasant... And only his dignity was truly harmed. Still, I'd asked Smiley to pass him some extra coins as we left.

After dinner, the Master asked me to stay behind, and join him by the fire.

"I'm very pleased, Tando," he said without ceremony, and he smiled. It was the first time I'd seen him do it, and it made him human – reduced him from loving father or master guildsman to just a regular person – and I found myself smiling back. I wondered what it would have been like to grow up with a father like this, instead of a mother sour from grubbing for every coin, and resenting every one I took from her.

"I think Elda enjoyed himself, Sir," I said modestly.

"I know he did." The smile was broader now. "He knows, of course, that it was always safe. But he enjoys the play." The Master turned serious. "He acts young, I know. It's his way of denying death, I think. But he's a bright boy. Almost as bright as you."

"I...," for once, I had nothing to say. "Thank you, Sir," I settled on at last.

"I mean it," he said. "You've done what I asked. You and Corak. You're all good children." I could hear a tremble in his voice, normally so controlled. "I wish... I wish..." He broke off and turned away. I could see the wet in his eyes glinting in the firelight.

"Thank you, Sir," I said, knowing I should go. I turned back at the door. "But, Sir." He kept his face turned away. "I... me and Corak. We're well off here, Sir, and we know it." I heard him scoff. "We're happy," I added, and slipped away to my chambers, leaving the Master behind me with sliver tracks running down his face.

From then on, we planned each escapade together, the Master and I. I would come up with ideas, strategies, campaigns, painstakingly, practically, clinically tailored to Elda's fading capacities, and my own. I drew up maps and plans until my hands failed me, and the Master took up the task with his own hands, until at times I thought his enthusiasm matched my own.

We went on scouting expeditions together, testing dangers, parsing risks, until I could no longer walk, and the Master went on his own, to report back to me in the evening, so that I felt like some grand general in the Mage Wars.

We'd even converted an evil mage, in the form of Darathar. He didn't take well to his role as my nurse, at first, but money and patience won him over, until he participated in our games as well as Smiley and Dwarf – with reserve and an eye roll to preserve their dignity, but with the same shouts and laughter as the rest of us.

Our company won battle after battle, quest after quest, even when, toward the end, they were restricted to the grounds of the manor itself.

It seemed months, but only five short weeks after the Defeat of Darathar, as it had come to be called, at the hands of the humblebracts, it came to an end, as we had all known it would.

I sat in my chair in Elda's bedroom, placed there by Darathar's surprisingly gentle hands. The shivers ran through me continually now, and I had trouble controlling my muscles. My heart and lungs worked at irregular speeds, and sometimes stopped altogether for a moment. It was this that would kill me in the end, that was killing Elda now.

"I've had a good time," he said to me now, in his labored way. Sitting beside him, arm wrapped around Elda's shoulders, was Corak. They'd given up any pretense in the last week, and Corak slept next to Elda every night. Or lay next to him, he'd told me. He lived in fear of sleeping and waking to find Elda dead. He'd stopped crying, too, and his thin face was gaunt and shadowed with dread. He smiled at me now, as much as he ever smiled, anymore.

"I'm glad," I told Elda. "Me too."

"It was good for all of us," he said. The childishness was gone from him now, and I saw him at last for who he truly was – a smart, kind boy, keenly aware of his own mortality and its effect on others. "For my father especially." A father, I knew who was out now scouting a new adventure that would never take place, and planning a funeral that would.

I nodded, with nothing left to say.

"You like him, don't you?" he asked, and slipped away.

As Corak found a new reservoir of tears, and Darathar slipped out to raise the alarm, I thought of the man who'd promised to care for me until my own death, now just weeks away, who'd shown the chances that love and privilege can buy, of what was possible without the grind of poverty to keep you down.

"We had fun," I said, and let my own tears flow as well.

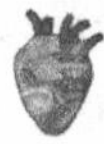

About the story

I put together an anthology, *Score*, in which the idea was that stories were to follow a common emotional score, with each author assigned to focus on a major and a minor emotion. For a number of reasons, I ended up writing two stories for the anthology myself. This one was meant to convey love and fun.

While I pretty quickly came up with the core structure of the guildmaster wanting his dying son to be happy. However, I wanted to subvert expectation a little by having the chosen companion grow to love the father instead of the boy himself.

When Dooryards First in the Lilac Bloomed

A Shy and Hidden Bird

The thrush led me astray. He with his puffed-out speckled chest and spindly legs, his impudent beak gated open and closed in song. He that stole my love, and left me desolate, cold, and lonely in the night; that secret, eremitic bird, with his liquid, taunting morning song. From high in the cedars, he sang my love away, and me awake.

In the week after the interment, he sang to me his joy of the spring, his pride in courtship, his love of life. It came to me as mockery, as cruel jest, delight in death. And so I rose and took my borrowed shotgun out in search of peace.

Peace was a thing the world had in plenty. Peace and harmony. Peace in our time. Peace in the Middle East, for gods' sake. A peace that brought stagnation; the death of ideas, of innovation, of discovery. A civilization of calm, incurious communities, slowly, contentedly sliding back into the ooze, progress a distant, forgotten goal, science a discarded fad.

We'd argued, in those awful, final days, when Isaac lay crumpled in his bed, bold voice withered by illness, his health spent on dawn treks through wet groves and fields after birdsong. In the hoarse whisper gifted him by that devil thrush, he claimed that peace was cause, not effect, that when we stopped our struggles, we lost our drive. Soldier, not warmonger, once young captain, now old lover, he held the change worthwhile — the slow and distant death of futures a small price for love — my love.

Love! What poets - cruel japesters - call this pain, this crushing, rending, mangling devastation of the soul. And that day, I went, gun in hand, to share my love with Isaac's favorite bird.

He led me on faint trails amidst dew-tipped spears of grass, through choked throats of bramble and thorn, flew his jagged way through foreboding mazes of spruce and pine - all Isaac's favored paths, that left him wet and happy and too tired to fight for health. I noted the cold no more than my lover had. I followed the thrush as he sang, whistled as I walked, false cheer a blind for cold, determined hate. For hours, I tracked him, always too far for my unpracticed aim, too quick for my grief-dulled wit. We twisted, turned, and twined until I lost my way, heedless of all but a small brown splash against green or blue or grey.

At last, he paused to rest, lighting softly near the top of a hill, a black silhouette against the sky beyond, with a silver cirrus cloud winding past his neck for scarf or noose. I knelt in the dark forest loam, fitting the gun stock smooth against my shoulder, my eyes never leaving that caustic fool in his feathered cloak of dun. He perched, bandy-legged, on a gentle curve of stone, fat little body framed by thin stalks and trunks, with delicate, pointed leaves wagging slyly from above.

As I cocked the hammer back, he fluttered his wings, and began to sing his hateful haunting song. On the breeze, the graceful, fragile scent of lilac, replacing the bitter tang of gunpowder with memories of sun, of shining hair, of picnics and of poetry, of death and of love. "Oh, Isaac," I breathed, and laid my gun aside.

I cursed the thrush as I dragged my heart up to his seat in the cemetery, that meager shelter ceiled with stiff sparse lilacs, floored with soft dark soil and a dust of bright green grass. I sat on the new bench, faced the new stone, its straight, true sides, its domed top. I read again the words Isaac had chosen, and I cried. Two words, one over the other, with a bar between. Like an equation, I'd joked. Exactly, he'd said, the equation for peace. Love over war.

"Love over War," I mumbled. "Love over war, you bastard bird." I faced the lilacs, planted one week back with my own hand. "*Fuck* you, thrush. Fuck you *and* your song." But he was gone, and I was alone.

Powerful, Western, Fallen Star

It was late, and I felt, now, the cold and the wet, on my hard stone bench. I was hungry, and thirsty, and my hands cramped from a day holding steel and death. The light was dimming, and up in the west, a shooting star streaked past my view. "Meteorite," I told Isaac, as always, and in memory he smiled, as if he'd never heard the word before, hadn't known already. I could almost feel his arm around me, still strong, still a bulwark against depression and despair. "Star," he'd insist. "We may not have progress anymore. But we still have dreams, and they're even better." Dreams worth their weight in birdsong.

No more stars appeared, and I closed my eyes. I was tired, and, thrush-peace or not, I still had to collect that damned gun. At least now I had my bearings, knew well the path from grave-garden to somber home.

I opened my eyes to a vertical whirl of color, like a violet mirage blossoming through desert air. I gripped the bench, seeking out its stalwart solidity as reassurance. I'd lost the habit of eating – occasional tremors a small price for the right not to think or plan. Tremors, not hallucinations, not visions. Weak body, not mind. Despite my anchor-bench, my lifeline to sanity, the vortex stayed, steadied, gradually cleared. Its lavender tones faded into the indigo of evening, thence to black of night, a cool dark circle of loss on the grave. And from its shadowed throat, the bright, meticulous tones of song.

A beautiful, subtle mystery of space or magic, and the universe used it to mock me.

"Fuck you too," I whispered, but I was drained, too empty and bare to put much heart into the words, my heart too worn to care. I closed my eyes, and the music stopped. No more cosmic mockery. Just a beautiful tear in space-time. I peeked from under one lid. Still a dark hole in the universe, with a pale violet filigree of nothingness at its edge. The music returned, a simple three note sequence, the first forceful, the second and third differing just a shade. They repeated, now elaborated, harmonized, embellished into a melody.

The space around the grave was immaculate, clear of stones; I'd cleaned it myself. I dug one cold hand into the ground at my feet, flung a clump of sod and soil at the black disk. It sailed through. A hole, after all. What else could have happened? My sod had likely surprised the hell out of some poor farmer in Uzbekistan. Or the moon, or Venus. Though maybe fewer farmers there.

My brain woke up at last, and with it what shreds of spirit I could gather. This was a miracle. A true marvel, a wonder of nature – or science. It occurred to me at last that music was not a natural phenomenon, but something made – crafted by living creatures. There was something or someone on the other side of that hole.

"Sorry," I said, for an opener. "Bad day. Do you come in peace?"

The response was a melody built of arpeggios, cadenzas, trills, drones – anything and everything, and all of it fit together. It held meaning layered on meaning, and I understood not one note.

I sat in silence, wanting more, not wanting to spoil the moment. Sunset painted the leaves with gold and scarlet, and a breeze warmed my sweat to salt. From the hole came a rich, loamy smell, fertile, lush, and verdant, like jasmine on dark spring earth. I wanted to go to it, to bury myself in its source and grow a new me, hale and hearty, healed of wounds, cleansed of faults, calm of mind. But I was afraid. *It's a hole,* my sane mind said. *Bloodthirsty aliens waiting to harvest your body, exchange it for pods.* It smelled good. *And it's on Isaac's grave.* A hole full of decaying matter and memory and hurt.

At last, I did what weak humans have always done with the unknown. I surrendered. I fell to my knees, held out my arms and said "Take me." *Eat me, pod me, harvest me. Make me better.*

Heart Shaped Leaves of Rich Green

The portal opened, or was uncovered. The black dissipated, like fog wafted away by a chance zephyr. Behind it, a broad lawn of golden yellow moss, with flowers of lime and rose, and trees dangling fruit in every shape and size. Banks of soil, blue as lapis lazuli, crumbled in banks and mounds, with a clear stream ramifying from pools and springs at every turn.

The song came again, in cellos, drums, and whispers. It called me, and I came. At the edge of Isaac's grave, I paused, unwilling to mark that still-loose soil, to mar its shroud of young grass. This was all I had of Isaac – soil and grass, stone and memory. Mostly memory. And paradise before me. But even as I hesitated, the door closed. Not black this time, but a growing net of branch and vine, delicate, yet dense, and covered with heart-shaped leaves in the purest emerald.

Too late! I stepped forward, heedless now of grave and grass alike. I flung myself into the gate, clung to the network, shook it. The vine were soft, and the perfume of those leaves was manna that calmed and soothed my hungry spirit. I pressed myself against them, but even as I did, I saw them wither, felt them crackle and snap beneath me. I drew back slightly, watched as they all fell away, broad feathers of jade fluttering to shatter and discolor on the ground.

The wood and vine of the network itself began to harden and flake, and its growth slowed. As it filled, it forced my fingers out, wakening me to their pain. As finger by finger slipped out of its net, I saw the skin seared and red. The pain was nothing next to the hurt in my chest at paradise regained and re-lost.

A single, heart-sized hole remained, at eye level, and through it, a glimpse of heaven. I pressed close again, but cautiously. Through the hole, I saw more vines, twining, lifting, forming into a shell of leaves. In it, a hard ebony oblong, like a river-worn stone. The leaves pushed it up and through the hole, and I reached for it anxiously. My fingers, stiff and swollen, failed to hold it, and it fell to the soil below. I scrabbled for it, mindless of the pain, and at last held it in one burning hand, felt the dark seed's cold solidity.

Through the port, vines swayed and danced, forming patterns that shifted from moment to moment in supple, elegant messages that said "We know you. We love you. Goodbye." The music slowed, saddened, and the violet edges of the portal thinned.

"Wait!" I cried. "Don't go." But the circle of the portal narrowed, violet reddening to pink and scarlet. I searched for something, anything to give in return. At last, I grabbed a spray of lilac with my free hand, snapped it, threw it through the portal and its port. "It's love," I said awkwardly as the portal contracted to nothing. "My love." Mine to give again, and lose again.

The Cedars Dusk and Dim

I go often now, to the little cemetery, with its single grave. The lilacs bloom and fade, share their sweet perfume to the world, with its message of delicate devotion. The grass on Isaac's grave is thick and full, with patches of bright bulbs in the corners – tulip, iris, daffodil, and one tall stalk of garlic with its sharp, irreverent spice.

I gathered what I could of alien plants and ash. I found two leaves largely intact, and carried them with slow, painstaking care to the house. I brought what scientists I could to examine them. Skeptical, but curious, they came in ones and twos and fives. They say the leaves are strange, unearthly. I keep the remains at home, and now there are sometimes a dozen strangers in the house. They bring their gels and microscopes, they write their learned papers, and they even speak of a small resurgence in science.

I've not yet shown my scientists the dark ovoid talisman that was my gift from the singers in the vortex. Is it a seed, a machine, a tool? I cannot say. I handle it at night, when my scarred hands give me pain. It soothes them and me, and sometimes I can sleep, to dream of birds and trees and wonder.

Who were these aliens? What were they? Was their realm itself toxic to me, and mine to them, or was it the portal that damaged us so badly? What did they intend, with their sweet perfumes and landscapes? Was it attack, seduction, communication, discovery, trade? Did my lilac gift survive, or my clod of earth? What did they make of it? I have no answers. What I have is the knowledge that our world has changed. In some small way, at least, that day among the lilacs reawakened our spirits, rekindled our yearning for knowledge. The flame is small, uncertain, but it burns. Progress, but if peace brought stasis, does progress bring war? I don't believe it.

In time, perhaps, I'll give over my black treasure, let the scientists examine and explore it, unearth its secrets. Perhaps not. There's a dark patch of soil at the center of Isaac's grave. I till it weekly with a little fork held awkwardly between my palms. Perhaps I'll plant my seed there, one day. Perhaps it will grow. An alien, should it survive. Or, less and more, a new doorway, a chance to try again.

I sit on my stone bench, in this cold, transparent night, reading Isaac's formula for peace. I trust, with my foolish, naïve spirit, that the aliens knew it too. Holding my dark secret, I gaze into space, or at lilac blossoms, or at a dark patch of fine rich earth. With the song of a hidden thrush in the air, I send this message with all my soul.

"Oh you with your green and leafy hearts, with your lilting tones and fair demesne, your promise of a new-returning spring. Come back."

About the story

This is, of course, based on the Walt Whitman poem, "When Lilacs First in the Dooryard Bloomed". The truth is, though, that I didn't know the poem that well, and when something I read referred to it, I was immediately struck with the idea of reversing the words of the title. I knew many of the lines, but went back and I read the whole poem again (or maybe for the first time) carefully. I used key lines to structure my own story.

Whitman's poem is about Lincoln, and that wasn't where I wanted to go, so I used his imagery more than his actual intent. I wanted a character that is dealing with the death of a loved one, but was aiming for something low-key and contemplative, like a Clifford Simak piece, I set it on an Earth that's both peaceful and stagnant, with somewhat incomprehensible aliens bringing hope.

Some Sun and Delilah

"I'll cut your hair," she said impulsively one evening. "You're getting shaggy, and far too blond with all this sun."

We were vacationing in the islands, trusting the fresh sea winds to bring life to stale hopes. We sat half-naked on limestone dust as soft as flour, and sifted it through our fingers. We'd made love as many times as there were shells strewn on the sand. It had brought back our glory days, when I was strong and confident, she sleek and clever. In our quiet cove under coconut palms, with the sly serenade of tropical wavelets tickling our feet, the heat fanned no flames, only set them flickering and uncertain, my small supply of virility too quickly exhausted, too slowly replenished. After only two days, happy banter ebbed with the sea, swirling away with manta rays and parrot fish to leave only silence and doubt and desperate measures.

She'd cut my hair only two weeks since, in the shabby Nairobi hotel that marked the start of our adventure of rediscovery. "To make the local girls jealous," she'd said at the time.

"Sure, why not?" I searched for a joke to match her mood. "Transform me to a handsome itinerant, searching out island rhythms."

"I'll show you island rhythms," she said, brushing one small, bikini-clad breast against my shoulder. "After your haircut."

In a chair on the porch of our bayside hotel cottage, I was hers to direct, to shape. "You're feeding stereotypes," I called as she gathered her tools. "Woman caring for man."

"As are you," she said. "Cave man with no couth." She pointed with her chin. "Wet your hair and come back."

A quick rinse later, I sat on the porch, cool water dripping down my thin, bare chest as she busied herself with scissor and comb. Little scraps of washed-out gold lay in shoals on my slightly sunburnt belly, and fell in clusters on her rich mahogany arms.

"I've been thinking," she said at last.

"Always good."

She folded my ear a little harder than I liked, and I winced at the thought of cartilage crumpling.

"I was talking with Angele, earlier." Angele and Pierre were the Rwandan couple to the left, our only neighbours aside from the Ukrainians who fought all night and spent their days in separate silence. I could see Yuri now, still out in his kayak in the bay, matching the hours of peace to the hours of light.

"Find anything out?" Angele was far younger than Pierre, and Rwandans were unlikely tourists so far from the mainland.

"She's his assistant, and they're on a study trip, investigating local government structures."

"Oh, come on." I took advantage of a break in the snipping to look around at Del. "Surely you don't believe that." We heard them having sex often enough, with a frequency and duration that gave us both food for thought.

"That's her story. He's the Deputy Minister, apparently." She stepped behind me and pushed my head forward. "Anyway, that's not the point. Angele said there's a guide who does a nice tour of local historical spots." She traded her scissors for a safety razor and scraped my tender, salt-crusted skin. "I thought we might check it out tomorrow."

Island history was low on my list of interests, but keeping Del happy was high. "Sure. Why not?"

"Apparently the hotel can set it up. If you don't want to, though, maybe we can go kayaking tomorrow." She stepped back to assess her handiwork. "Or you can go with Yuri."

I smiled as dashingly as I could. "I don't know. Historical tour with beautiful brunette all to myself, or vigorous exercise with bulky Ukrainian gangster. Hard choice."

"I'm serious," she said. "If you don't want to come..." I could see that it was important to her, that she was trying as hard as I to avoid those awkward silences, the long moments of broken conversation between bouts of sex.

"I do," I assured her with a kiss on the hand. "And thanks for the haircut. What did you say happens afterward?" I drew her down toward me and kissed her sun-flaked lips before taking her inside to make her happy.

In the morning, we rose early for a quick swim in the shallow bay, threading through the beds of seaweed, trying to avoid encountering the little sharks more frightened than we, and the stingrays hiding under the sand. A game of tag turned quickly into a clinging, fumbling roll, and we sped back to shore and bed. Sex was best early in the day, when it was still fresh, when our hopes sprang newborn from dreams of glad repletion.

After she came, we lay for a while together, my hand still trapped in the warmth between her legs, my face resting on her shoulder.

"So," I said when she sighed and stirred at last. "How do we find this guide lady?" I'd thought of pretending ignorance, letting her, sated, ignore the plan. But she'd been sated other mornings also, as well as I could manage.

She smiled and rolled to face me. "I'm so glad you remembered." She laid an arm on my chest. "I know it's not really your thing, but I thought ..." She'd apparently thought something too dangerous to name, and changed it mid-sentence. "You know. New places, new things."

"Old historical sites." It was a joke, though, and we showered together, soaping each other in silent search of a resurgence that didn't arrive.

"Just as well," she said, rinsing. "I told the hotel we'd meet her at ten." I looked at my watch. We had just enough time to dress. I carefully didn't consider when she might have had time to arrange the meeting.

At the oversized thatched hut that served as reception, our guide was waiting. She was small and a pleasant light brown, with tightly curled grey hair, and faintly Asian eyes that widened when she saw us. Better prospects than she'd envisioned, perhaps.

"Bonjour," I said in my best rusty French. "Parlez-vous anglais?"

"Of course, monsieur. I am an accredited guide. Your French is excellent, but we can speak English if you prefer."

“Of course we’ll speak English,” Del decided. “He’s just showing off.” She extended a hand. “My name is Del.”

“Mine is Carinne. And this must be Sam.” Her right eye, on the far side from Del, winked at me. “You see? I do my research as well. The owner here is an old friend.”

We spent the morning touring plain, whitewashed churches and research stations, squat municipal buildings and decrepit statues. Despite Carinne’s best efforts, I was bored, and I doubt Del was more enthralled, but we persevered until the tour ended on a narrow tarmac street with open air cafés and restaurants to one side, fine white sand to the other.

“Here I leave you,” declared Carinne. “At the best restaurant for you on the island.” She gestured to one of the indistinguishable restaurants, its white plastic tables stained and scored by years of careless diners.

“Thank you, Carinne. It’s very kind, but ... we’re vegetarians. Very strict.” Seaside places, in my experience, serve fish, fish, and more fish.

“I told you, Mr. Sam. I do my research. The proprietor here serves the best vegetarian meals in town.” That twinkle again. “Perhaps the only ones. He is my good friend, and you may trust him. Now come,” she ushered us through a gap in the low whitewashed wall. “Jean! Les étrangers ont arrives. Apporte les aliments exotiques.” She smiled at me.

“But you must join us, Carinne,” said Del.

“No, Ms. Del. I cannot. It is very kind, of course, but ...”

“Never mind that,” Del insisted. *Why not?* I thought. Carinne had done her best, and I didn’t grudge her a little extra. It might help us avoid the awkwardness of a tip, and I gave Del silent credit for the idea.

The food was excellent — grilled vegetables, a salad of seaweed and beans, and a spicy curry of coconut milk and nuts poured over rice. Jean, the rail-thin black proprietor and cook, bustled merrily back and forth with dishes, pickles, and drinks, until at last Del insisted he join us as well.

We told abbreviated versions of our lives, and listened to their talk of island scandal, until, bellies bulging, we sat back, vainly trying to find room for delicious little cups of some white jelly, with bits of mango. It tasted of coconut and mint.

"So," asked Jean at last. "How was your tour?"

I tried desperately to remember the names of even one of the sites.

Del, more self-assured, said "The churches were lovely."

"Bah," said Jean. "The usual spots. Is this the best you can do, Carinne?"

She shrugged. "This is the tour. I am sorry if it is not interesting."

"Not at all," I said hurriedly.

Jean cut me off. "No one is interested in these things."

"It was very interesting," I insisted. "The botanical research station, for example, where they're growing the, um, ..."

"Coco de mer," offered Del. The nut looked somewhat like a woman's buttocks from one side, and the other side looked even less like a woman's front.

Jean sniffed. "For tourists. They love it. The nut has no uses, otherwise."

"It makes good bowls," offered Carinne. "And the jelly from young nuts is very good." She gestured at the dessert bowls before us.

"And it's an aphrodisiac," Jean admitted.

"Where can we get more?" I jumped in, joking.

"Very rare," Carinne said, shaking her head. "Jean has been generous with you."

"I give my guests what they need," he said. Did I imagine a sympathetic glance in my direction? "What about you?" He caught Carinne's eye and held it.

"Me." It was clear that she knew what he meant.

"Yes, you. Why not show them something really interesting, for once?" The weight of a hidden message was not lost on any of us.

Carinne considered, looking from me to Del to the dessert with a troubled brow.

"Why not, Carinne?" Del asked. "Is there more to show us? Please do."

"Are you sure?" She looked searchingly into Del's eyes. "Perhaps. But you," she turned her keen gaze to me. "What is it you long for?"

"Something new," I said glibly. "Or old." In truth, another day of boring monuments was not my idea of a holiday, but clearly the mystery had caught Del's interest, and for that, I was willing to spend a few more dull hours growing blisters. Plus, we might end up here for lunch again, and that seemed an excellent idea.

Carinne bit her lip, but Jean nodded, and she gave in. "Very well. Tomorrow afternoon, then. There is a temple. It is very old, very broken. You may not find it interesting."

A temple, at least, would be a break from cinder block administrative buildings, and equally stolid churches.

"It sounds lovely," said Del. "Tomorrow, then,"

Del and I left Carinne at the restaurant, and walked slowly, happily down the narrow streets to our hotel. We were silent, mostly, but we held hands, and for the first time in a while, it felt good.

That night, it felt more than good. I managed twice, three times — a record! Then four and five, before we sank exhausted into sleep. In the morning, we were sore but willing, and after slow, tender lovemaking, we spent the early day drowsing and snuggling as we hadn't done for months. After a perfunctory lunch, we moved to the open air bar, and sat drinking cool, fresh juice until Carinne arrived.

"You are ready?" she asked.

"Ready," Del declared for the two of us.

"Ready," I echoed, remembering the night. "Ready. And maybe dinner at Jean's, eh?"

Carinne shook her head, serious. "Perhaps. But too much coco de mer... It is not good for everyone. Maybe not for you." Was my inadequacy so clearly on display for all to see? I bridled, but Carinne put her hand on my arm. "It is no bad thing," she said. "The more one takes, the higher the price." I was unsure if she referred to the law of supply and demand, or some metaphysical mumbo jumbo, but her eyes were kind, and I chose to let it go.

"Let's be off, then," I said to cover my irritation. "Ruined temples, here we come."

We set out on foot, up the main road into the coastal hills. I insisted on carrying Carinne's bag full of supplies, and she handed it over with a shrug — a peace offering of sorts, perhaps; a nod to my virility.

We turned off the road to a broad path, then a narrow one, then a faint trail in the jungle. Around us, lianas hung from jellyfish trees and palms.

"Look," said Del, pointing to the side. "Coco de mer." Indeed, they grew more frequent the further we went, until we stood in a veritable forest of palms.

"So much for rarity," I said. "Maybe we can point Jean to this place." Del reached back to squeeze my hand.

Soon after, the trail debouched into a small clearing with a short drop to the beach one side, and rock on the other. On the inland side, a single stained stone pillar poked drunkenly toward the sky.

"Temple, I'm guessing," I offered, to fill the silence. It didn't look like much. There was the one pillar, a few tumbled blocks, and a curtain of vines. There was no sign of a portico or roof; just the remains of these stones.

"Is there an inside?" Del asked. Without waiting for an answer, she strode over to the ruins.

Beside the single pillar, vines hid not rock, but a dank, dismal emptiness. It smelled of urine, dust, and guano.

"After you," I motioned to Carinne, before remembering that if there were torches to be found, they must be in her pack, still tight against my back. Del had already plunged into the darkness, though, and Carinne stepped in after her.

"Give me your hand," she said, reaching forward for Del's and back for mine. I took it, not wanting to let them head off without me into the dark. There was a small delay as she pushed ahead of Del, and we all traded hands.

As my eyes adjusted to the dim light, I saw that the entry was lined with rough stone slabs, and looked up with trepidation to see the same just over my head. "Is it safe?" I asked, scuffing the toe of my shoe into the silt of the floor.

"Safe?" asked Carinne, starting forward again. "I think we are past safe."

"What? What the...?"

"Oh, man up, Sam. It's just a little darkness."

I bit down on my response and shuffled forward, my shoes sliding past unknown objects as we twisted and turned into a tunnel. Probably the bones of small animals. Or of unmanly men, frightened of the dark.

"Oh," exclaimed Del from before me. A moment later, I could see a faint grey glow from walls that seemed to stretch far higher than before. "It's beautiful," she said. "Like pearls."

"Very dirty pearls," I said, telling myself to enjoy her pleasure, but unable to make myself do it.

In the dim light, I could see her shake her head at this evidence of philistine character, but she said nothing.

The glow grew stronger, and I could see that it came from a coarse white coating high on the walls.

"Like mother of pearl," Del said, though I could see no such resemblance.

Now that there was light, however faint, I could see that the walls had changed from stone slabs to raw stone, scraped and broken in places to widen the passage. Stalactites dripped down from the ceiling, or formed veins down the walls. It formed a sort of natural temple in itself, and I wondered why it wasn't better known. It was certainly a better tourist attraction than the dumpy town hall.

At the far end of this natural hall, we entered another tunnel. It was short; after only two quick turns, we emerged into the blinding outdoor light. My eyes slowly, painfully adjusted, to see a lush, green paradise of fruit and flowers. I felt a sense of discontinuity, as if I'd stepped into an entirely different world. Not dark and close, like the thick palms of the outer island, this land was light and open, with lawns of moss, and benches of smooth stone shaded by broad yellow blossoms on tall, pale stalks.

Half-hidden by leaves, like a mixer at god's nudist colony, group upon group of beautiful people. Young, old, fat, thin, pale, dark, but all with an ineffable sense of grace, an almost tangible aura of perfection. They were people you just wanted to be with, full of smiles and warmth and a twinkle in the eyes.

Del was already among them, chatting, shaking hands, being hugged — a friend among old friends she'd only just met. I watched with stupefaction as she passed among them, casually shedding bits of clothing as she went. A hat here, a shoe here, handing off her blouse as if it were the most natural thing in the world. By the time she was naked, she was hidden by the crowd. I yearned to go to her, half envious, half jealous, held back by fear and, I slowly realized, by Carinne's hand in mine. Slowly, unwillingly, I looked toward her.

Our guide stood just inside the cave. In contrast to perfection, she seemed a crumpled gargoyle of nut-brown parchment and angled bone. With one gnarled clutch of twigs, she held close to the rough stone of the rock face, as if mooring herself against a winter storm. Her fragile form seemed now a caricature of delicacy, a mockery of beauty drawn by the cruelest of artists, a satirist of poise and elegance.

"Stay," she said, pulling on my hand with her own frail fingers. "Stay. This is not for you."

I stared at her, uncomprehending. Here was Eden recreated, Shangri-La amidst the ocean, Arcadia discovered and Pan no doubt among the crowd. Making love to my own love, no doubt.

"Let her go," Carinne said. "She will come back."

I shook my head and pulled away, stepped out into the warm and gentle sun.

"Stay," she called again, her voice thin and harsh and bereft of all command. "You will regret it."

It could have been Cassandra's catchphrase, for all the attention anyone has ever paid those words. I turned away to follow Del, to join or rescue her.

I stepped toward the nearest of the golden people, a short, plump man with skin so black it shone like obsidian, and a woman blonde as gold and twice as bright. They smiled and took me in their arms. I felt a man among men, with hands as strong as oak and capable of any task. We walked arm in arm among the crowd. I spoke with the flowing eloquence of my best moments, said the right things at the right times, never stumbled, never lost for words. The men looked up to me, respected me. The women pressed against me, fluttered their eyes, laughed at my jokes, rejoined with cutting repartee always clever, never cruel. We competed amongst each other, and I won as many matches as I lost, all in good grace, all in good spirits. When we made love, it was a natural consequence, the graceful conclusion of one impish contest or another. When it was over, there were no hidden glances, no bitter, unsatisfied looks, only utter contentment, and a fluid shift to other topics, other activities. We talked, we laughed, we sang. We ate fruit sweet and tart and refreshing all at once, drank the milk of coconuts, or water as pure as the sky was blue. It lasted forever.

In every tale, forever has an end, the moment when the infinity of now becomes contained, forced back from eternity by the boundaries of tomorrow and of yesterday.

One day, or night, or dawn, as we composed eddas on the stars and moon and sun, a woman curled in between a male form and a female one, lay across a lap, soft breasts against soft thigh. She looked at me with warm eyes of jade, and smiled. I lost my place, but the crowd carried on, taking my long verse for its own, continuing and reshaping it, making my stumble into a victory.

"Hello Sam," she said.

"Del." I knew her now, and though she shone with the grace of all these other gods, she was the same.

"Are you happy, Sam?" She reached out and stroked my hair. "At last?"

And though I had sung of happiness moments before, of a sudden I was not. I was cold and stiff and dry, and fear pressed in on me.

"Let's go home," she said. As if home were more than bills and work and strain and a squalid flat.

I heard her cry behind me as I ran, the click of my bones setting the metre for the sound of my name, repeated over and over in diminishing echoes. I plunged through a crowd of strangers, in search of contentment. I lost myself in women, holding them in brief, brutish spasms that left me drained and empty, left them frowning as they turned away in search of other partners. The men took me in, shook my hands with grips that made me wince, talked in codes I was always slow to decode, turned me away for better companions. I slaked my thirst with water that tasted of silt, ate green fruit already riddled with rot. At last I slept.

When I woke, my thoughts were slow and painful, and my mouth tasted of decay. I stretched in painful jerks. Beneath me, sharp corners of flint gouged loose skin, sent flurries of gravel down to the muddy rill below. Above me on either side stretched crags of stone hung with scraggly bushes. And when I rose, not far away, Carinne and Del watching with compassion and contempt.

I gathered my clothing, torn and scattered among the jagged boulders of the ravine, fished one shoe from a puddle, the other from a thornbush. As I dressed, the women chatted quietly until at last I stood before them, the barest semblance of a man.

We spoke little as we traversed the tunnels, Carinne's torch leading the way. She carried her own pack. I took Del's hand in the grand central chamber, and she let it hang there, limp and distant until we came once more to the dark, salty night of the exit. There, she squeezed once and let go. We walked home in silence, letting Carinne go her way with no more than a nod.

We kept apart for the remaining days of our vacation. Some days, I went out with Yuri and his kayaks. Some days Del did. On those days I sat alone on our little porch, overlooking the sea. Yuri's pretty brunette came by once or twice, but when I didn't respond, she left me alone. Pierre and I talked, sometimes, but I knew little about African politics, and he had little else to say.

I went back to the temple, of course. When Del was out, or early in the morning, or late at night. You know what I found. Sometimes nothing. Sometimes the cave had no exit, sometimes no entrance. Sometimes it was a den of dust and dry bone. Once it was full of island hooligans who beat me and robbed me and threw me to the beach below the cliff. When I crawled home at last, Del said nothing, only bandaged my wounds with quick efficiency, and went to take tea with Angele.

I spoke with Carinne one more time, at Jean's little restaurant. She just shook her head. "It was for Del," she said. "It was suited to her. A dream and a release. For people like you it is only danger and obsession and ruin."

I told Del those words, and she shrugged. "You hold too closely, Sam. You're a man of infatuations." She took my hand gently, looked me in the eye as she cut her losses. "Be happy, Sam. Next time."

After we left the islands, we didn't see each other again. She took her things from my flat, and I didn't search her out. I had moments of sorrow, moments of rage, of violence. The other tenants, cowards all, asked that my lease not be renewed. I left the landlord my wreck of a home, and moved.

Here in the north, the waves are tall and cruel, and the beach is cold black grit. Hard work has made me strong, so strong. I lay my head upon the sand, and it mingles with my long, graying hair. When I comb it out, the sand forms stiff, crumbling patterns on my hearth, mountains and canyons of piled, isolated grains, touching but ever separate. I throw them in the fire, but they never melt into glass. Tomorrow, though, I will turn up the heat. I will comb my hair and wear my best clean clothes. I will go to the town, and sit in the library or the teahouse or the pub, and I will try to make a friend. If the gods are with me, I will see whether strength can build as well as destroy.

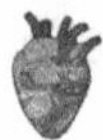

About the story

I wanted to write a story in the style of Richard Cowper (John Murry), and was specifically inspired by his novelette "Incident at Huacaloc", about a couple who visit an old temple with troubling results. I stole those elements and some of the feel of the story, though the rest is quite different. I don't remember now whether I already had the title lying around or it came along with the idea. I seldom address sex in my stories, but here I made it central to the narrator's sense of self. Details of the temple itself are invented, but the general location draws vaguely from a wonderful trip to the Seychelles many years ago when we lived in central Africa and figured it was as close as we'd ever get. Sadly, the vegetarian food wasn't as good as in the story. And I don't recall the coco de mer having any effect. But the snorkeling was beautiful.

Crying in the Salt House

The Salt House is built on tears, not of them. That is only a little joke the Bracque like to play. They tell to visitors that the blocks of pure, clear salt are the crystallized tears of children, and the rougher, grayer stones are the tears of the parents who lost them.

It is not true. Had it been, we should all have wandered the halls with little vials strapped to our faces, and the House would be much larger than it is.

The visitors believe, because they look for romance, and because they are disappointed. They come from far away, and they find only a squat gray house with slumping walls of stone. It is not the limpid, lucent castle they found in their heads. Some of them go away without seeing inside. They are content with the tawdry, gaudy mock-ups put up by the Braque, accurate in every notion, incorrect in every detail.

It is true that the House is no beauty. It stands on the barren salt pan where once a sea pooled shallow among low hills and far mountains. The land is parched and harsh, and even the

Bracque live on the fringes, at the mouths of creeks that once were rivers, before the land lifted and shifted, before the sea drained dry. Now all that is left is the flat seabed, crusted with salt to a child's waist height. I know, for I have stood in it.

Nothing lives on the salt. It is why *he* was sent here from the green cities of the south. They condemned him to die slow and lonely, because they had not the will to kill him quickly. Instead of dying, he built the House. He is a resourceful man, our master, and a stubborn one. It will stand him in good stead.

The salt of the seabed is not suited for building. It is thick, but friable, and it melts in the rain. The House is built instead of evaporite stones from the northern hills, mined by free Bracque, and by prisoners from the south. The stones are dark and dreary, with streaks of white running down their faces from moisture. They melt also, but more slowly, so that the roofs and crenels of the House are rounded and tired, but whole.

The Bracque say he deliberately built the House from mined salts as a gesture to his enemies. They say much and know little. The master is a man of the future, a man of clear vision. He does not think of the south, except in terms of business.

When I first came to the salt, I was too young to think, except of the present. My father had been fined and then sentenced for improper solicitation, which means turning down the advances of the nobility. "It is noble to think always of yourself," he told me. I did not know the meaning of irony, at the time.

In fact, it is in the nature of people to think always of themselves. It is the essence of survival, I think. Looking beyond oneself is a risk. Our master looked deeper and further than most, and see him now. They come to see him every day.

My father died in the mines. It is a slow death, and painful, choking in the cold salt grime, but it seemed rapid to me. One day he left and told me to wait. Another day they came to tell me he had died and that I had become a ward of the master. Nothing changed, except that after another year I ceased to wait.

Waiting is an art we know much of, here in the salt – waiting for rain, for revenge, for release. We wait still, spinning around the House like the world spinning on its axis, leaning sometimes one way, sometimes another, but never changing position. The master waits with us, and often I think he is the only one who knows what for. Perhaps we only wait for him to tell us.

When he was exiled, he used the last of his influence to purchase a salt license, a right to provide the pure, fine salt that sparkles like diamond across southern tables, and lies like dust upon their dishes.

We scoop it up with shovels in the salt pan, deep in the interior, where the Bracque have not fouled it with their wastes and their fires. When I came to the House, I worked as a holder, holding open the mouths of the soft, tightly woven fine-sacks for a filler to shovel salt dust into. It is easy work, but hard on the body. Many of the children die of it, never learning how to guard their eyes, and noses, and not least the ears.

"Take off your shirt," my filler told me, on my first morning. I did, because though my father had warned me against disrobing, he had also warned me what would come if I fought against authority.

"Always choose the lesser of two evils," he told me. It is not so easy a choice as it seems.

"Small, aren't you?" the filler Rula asked, and indeed her lean form towered above me, runnels of sweat already etched into a layer of salt along knotted muscle, though her torso was closely covered. "You'll grow." She took my shirt from me, and tore strips from its tail. I had no other, nothing in fact but loose trousers I wore with a string to hold them up. "Here," she said, giving me back a tatter of cloth.

I took the remains of my shirt, put my arms through it, and let the yoke settle. My belly was cool where where the shirt ended in ragged threads. "Now these," she said, and plugged my ears with cloth when I stared at her in bafflement. "And the nose. And around the eyes." She thrust a soft sack into my hands, showed me how to hold it open. "Never," she said, "never open your eyes until I say so." And for years I did not, though within two years I was a filler myself, and Rula was gone to the House. It is easiest, sometimes, to have a reason for not seeing.

As a holder and filler, I did not live in the House itself. I lived with Rula and the other prisoners' children in a Bracque encampment at the edge of the seabed. The Bracque were foul and coarse, but they worked hard enough when they cared to. Near as many of them died in the master's mines as did prisoners, though they were better paid. Minding children was easy work in comparison. Besides, where would we go, with seabed to the north and west, rocks to the east, and nothing but civilization to the south?

A Bracque matron named Erna would march us to the salt pit every day, and set us to work.

Occasionally, a boy or girl would be tasked to fetch more fine sacks, or the coarser bags we packed those into, or a crew would be set to hauling a wagonload south to the encampment. Those walk-tasks were coveted assignments, and Erna liked to see us scuffle for them. The walk-work was hard; the salt tore at our toughened feet, and the wagon traces sank into our muscles like wire, but out in the open, we could breath. "The air is only 10% salt," walkers would joke, an improvement on the clouds of salt that surrounded fillers and holders like a caustic mist.

Eventually, I graduated to filler, alongside Rula. We could not talk during the day, for if you opened your mouth, the salt would come in, and then you would cough, and breathe in more, and you would collapse there in the salt, and the holders would be made to drag you out.

We talked at night in the camp, when it was too dark to dig. The Bracque had a little stream they used for drinking water, and Rula insisted we bathe in it every week. We would walk up into the hills a little, where a low ridge hid the Bracque's low huts and our own shabby lean-tos. There Rula would insist I turn my back, and keep guard. I earned my keep, for though she was too young to have any curves, there were always those wanting to look, or to tell lies about what we did there together. It is a strange thing that so many of us seek out only what is forbidden, and turn away from what is before us every day.

One night, as I took my turn bathing, and Rula watched over me, she told me that she had reasoned out the way of Erna and her tasks. "She does not choose the one who fights the best, but the roughest, the most desperate. The most grateful." And once a week, the most attractive; that was understood, but Rula was too gawky to be chosen for sex.

"Erna is a bully," she said, and since coming to the salt, I had learned something of bullying. Bullying is to take something from someone so that they hurt, not because you want it. I think we are all the bully at times. "When next there is a walk-task," Rula said, "make a fuss. Pretend to fight me, but I will let you win. Then Erna will choose you, because you are small and you have beaten me. You must try to cry when we fight." We all cried all the time from the salt, as if it were the only way to rid our bodies of an excess of the stuff.

"I will not cry if you do not hit me," I said, to show tough, because Rula was a hard girl, and she would not cry from only frustration or loss.

"Oh, I will hit you. And you must hit me as well." She stopped her talk to look and listen for no one there. "But you must make sure not to hit me here." She gestured toward her midriff, where ribs joined belly.

"I will not hit you anywhere," I said, for Rula was my one protector, and if I hit her, whom would I turn to?

"No, you must. I insist on it, boy," and she smiled to play the noble with me. "Only not here. I have ... I have an injury here. A growth of sorts." I could see that it hurt her, and I was surprised that she hid the pain so well, digging in the salt. "But you must wrestle with me, and hit me as if you were my brother. Are we agreed?"

I agreed, though I had no brothers, and no sisters either, and I did not know how to hit them.

On the next task day, Rula and I put on a good performance, and she fetched up with a bloody nose, crying for real from the pain of the salt we had rolled in. I, triumphant, ignored the ache in my belly where Rula's elbow had dug in hard, and stood up for Erna to call me. In my nervous excitement, I forgot to cry, and I sometimes wonder how things might have been different had I been less hard.

Erna did not call my name. I have never been sure whether she saw through Rula's childish ploy, or whether, true to her nature, Erna simply chose to flaunt her power by defying expectations. In either case, I learned an important lesson about subtlety. She called instead to Rula, where she knelt in the white salt dust, pretending defeat. Rula flicked her eyes sideways to me, and I shrugged. The ploy had worked, and if Rula were the one to benefit from her own idea, that was surely right.

She never came back. Often in life, we learn the important matters too late. Before Rula, I never had a friend that I can recall. Not until I lost her did I know that she was friend to me and more, and the knowledge set in my heart a pang that has never quite left it.

After two weeks, I bathed by myself, and cut my hair with a borrowed knife, and caught Erna's eye. I learned, at the expense of a tedious evening licking salt off the more noisome portions of her spare figure, that Rula had been taken into the Salt House, to serve there.

When my service to Erna was done, I rose in the moonlight, and walked to the edge of the seabed. There, across the flat, white plain, the House swelled, a small, dark protuberance like the nipple on Erna's breast. My first imagination of Rula in the house is thus always tangled with

Erna's gross desire. It is a matter of some frustration to me.

I went to the House myself within the year. My night with Erna paid also for one trip to collect sacks, and the others I won by chance. I let Erna bully me without complaint, and she lost the pleasure in it.

On my first visit, I came no nearer to the House than its storeroom, a squat gray extrusion of evaporite along the House's northern face. To the west of the House, a bed of flat tiles held a foul green liquid. It smelled of sewage, and so the storesgirl confirmed it to be.

"It has to go somewhere," she said. "At least here it dries and blows away." She wore tunic and trousers that came close to fitting, but she was a greasy, slovenly type, for all the fancy clothing.

"Never mind," I replied, and then, with as much confidence as I could muster, "Do you know Rula? Is she here? Is she well?"

Her eyes widened at the name. "I must go."

I grabbed her by the arm, greatly daring, for she was easily twice my age, and large with it.

"Let me go," she cried, and batted away my arms. I grabbed her again, as it was clear she knew something of Rula, and I meant to have it out of her if I had to hit her. "Let me go," she cried, and set her knee in my groin. It would have hurt me more in a few years, but it was bad enough, and I had only the will to grasp her ankles from where I lay on the salt. She kicked and stomped, but I held on to her as she shuffled toward the storeroom.

"Tell me," I cried, getting my breath back at last.

"What's this?" An old man of fifty or more, thin like sticks held together by clay, had emerged from the House. "Piro! Explain yourself. And you, boy, get up."

"He grabbed me, Nerk" she muttered. "And would not let go. He has gone wild, out in the ... out there."

"Are you wild, boy? So wild that you must be dragged on the salt rather than walk?" He jerked his head to Piro, and she slunk back toward the door.

"Well, boy? If you would enter the storeroom, you must answer to me, or I am no storesman, and as I am Nerk, and Nerk is a storesman, I must be one."

I had difficulty following his talk, but I covered it in climbing up from the salt and bowing to him. "My apologies, storesman Nerk," for so I thought him to be. "I sought only to learn the whereabouts of my friend, Rula, who came here some weeks since."

"Ah, Rula. And you are her friend, you say?"

"I am." Though it seemed a troublesome thing to be, I stood by it, for that is what friendship is for, and I had little else.

"A dedicated one, it seems. Well, I shall keep my eye on you. In any case, yes, she is here. A scrappy young thing, much like yourself, perhaps. So perhaps she will serve, in time. Or perhaps not." A shadow crossed his taut face, and he smiled it away. "We shall see. Indeed we shall. But now, go your way, boy, and leave our Piro here alone."

And so I left, smelling the House's foul stench all the way back to the salt pit, for the wind had changed, and it bore with it my wonder at the House's strained atmosphere, but also my satisfaction, for it seemed Rula had made a mark for herself already.

My next few months in the salt pit taught me little. I filled sacks, avoided bullies, and kept happy knowing that Rula had found a place in the House. On occasion, Erna assigned me a walk-task, more from boredom than purpose, for I did nothing to gain her attention. On every visit to the House, I asked for Rula, and on every occasion, Nerk came out to eye me and to tell me she was well.

On my fourth trip to the House, Nerk told me to stay. He put me to work in the sack room, sewing the coarse bags that held the fine-sacks of salt powder.

"It's all you're good for," he said. "Show me your hands." I held out fingers cracked and callused by three years of living and shoveling salt. "As I thought. Maybe in a month or two, we can set you on the fine work. Or not. You've a look about you."

I looked about me. The exterior of the Salt House had been gray and dark, but for windows of stacked, translucent blocks. On the inside, the House lived up to its name. Save for pillars of light gray evaporite, the walls and floor and ceiling, were salt, as indeed was every surface. Not the dusty, brittle salt of the seabed, but blocks of hand-smoothed white and gray, veined in places with yellow, blue, and purple that I had never, in my years on the salt pan, imagined.

I learned with time that the purity of the salt rose with the level of the house, so that the highest floor, where the master worked, was built of blocks transparent as ice, and just as smooth. Here in the bowels of the House, wondrous as it seemed to me, were the dregs of the mine, the blocks just salt enough to merit the term.

I sat on the salt block floor, looking at these wonders, and wishing for someone to talk to about it. "Where is Rula?" I blurted to Nerk, as he turned from showing me the spot under a shelf where I was to sleep with the other sewers.

"Never you mind," he said shortly, and took me off to show me the other sewer. "We drain off the liquid here, see, let it out through these pipes. Left for west, right for east, depending on how the wind's blowing. Evaporates right away, it does, and the residue blows off across the salt pan. The solid stuff we put in a wagon, haul it out to the Bracque. They put it on their food, or something."

It was all made of salt. Even the pipes and the cesspit, foul as they were, were made of ducts and blocks of grey evaporite.

"Does it not melt?"

"Course it does, eventually. This evaporite, stuff, though, it's not regular salt. Probably mostly rock, I guess. Takes a while to leak. When it does, though, that's a task, replacing all this. More often upstairs, of course. Do that pretty often. More true salt up there."

I worked in the storeroom for half a year. My fingers caught on the rough fabric of the canvas bags, and my thick-callused fingers fumbled with needle and thread, until Nerk despaired of teaching me to sew, and set me to polishing floors instead. I wandered the lower floors with a small bucket and a soft cloth, wiping up the dust that constant foot traffic wore off the salt slabs, and cleaning my rag in water that slowly turned to brine. After an hour, my hands would tremble at the thought of one more rinse, one more wring working the salt into tiny cracks in my hands that would never close. By the end of the day, the tears would come, and leave their salt in the cracks along my cheeks and mouth. At that, I had more access to water than most, and I washed with it as well as I was able before starting my morning rounds. The water was already fourth hand by then, having been used by Nerk, and the chamberlain, and perhaps a guest or even the master before that. During a long day in the salt pit, I would have drunk it without question. Here in the Stone House, we had water enough for drinking and bathing both, some of us. It warmed me to think that Rula too could bathe daily, wherever she might be in the upper ranges of the House.

It was not for want of trying that I did not find her. For all its beauty, the House was oppressive, its still interior a cold contrast to dusty chaos of the salt pit. Despite the cleaner air, it was almost as silent. Among the servants, we seldom spoke, and with each new arrival to a room, talk paused while all evaluated what had been said, and what might have been heard. I could not tell, at first, what subjects to avoid. It was only with time that I understood the fear was not of any subject, but of being noticed at all. By the time I knew this, I had already caught Nerk's eye, though no ill seemed to come of it.

In the storerooms, for there were more than one, we worked at our menial tasks, occasionally graduating to larger positions. Like me, the other children had no family, and no thought beyond their daily work. Unlike me, Nerk paid them no special attentions. "You've a look about you," he would say, especially when I pressed him about Rula. The children knew no more. "Gone in the salt," was all they would say of her. To a boy surrounded by salt, that meant little.

I used my cleaning tasks to search her out, walking near-invisibly into the guest areas, and more noticed into those used by servants. It was in the kitchen I had my first clue. There was a boy there not much older than me. He seemed friendly as he darted here and there for spices and provender. He was a striking child, with sandy skin and hair a thick, wild tangle of tight brown curls. One day, he let fall a chunk of brown crystal, and mimed putting it in his mouth.

I did not need for salt, but it was a small cost for a kindly smile in that sad house, and I complied. I had never tasted sugar before. I savored the memory that evening, and all the next day, and the week after, going so far as to surreptitiously lick some of the browner floor stones. They were salt.

When I next had a chance to enter the kitchen with my rag, I asked after my new friend. "In the salt," was all they said, and the usually quiet kitchen stilled further until I left.

"It's a price," Nerk told me that evening. He shifted his feet as he sat in the storeroom. His gaze, so often sharp and penetrating, had become obtuse and vague, eyes shifting from shelf to shelf around the room. "It's a price, for what we have, what we all have." His eyes flicked to me momentarily. "And we all pay. Remember that. We all pay the price, one way or another." He would say no more.

Nerk set me to carrying messages and small bundles of supplies, so that I traveled a broader reach within the House, and even spoke on occasion to the upper servants. The task came with clothes that fit, a shirt and trousers of barely-patched white cotton. I walked straight and proud and blind in my finery while the other low-servants slunk beside the walls. Pride is like the sun shining in your eye. The more you have, the brighter your path appears, and the fewer of its pitfalls you see.

After several months, my kitchen friend was back. I stopped short when I passed one day, to see him somberly chopping a row of carrots. I slipped through the door and smiled.

"Hello," I said, as he continued to chop.

He nodded. His face was the same gold hue as before, but lacked for sparkle, for vivacity.

"You're back," I added. "From the salt." Whatever that might be.

If his face had been still before, now it was flat as the salt pan outside, his eyes as dead as the fish we sometimes found in the bottom layers of the pit. He turned his white, staring gaze on me, then turned away, sweeping carrots into a heavy bowl. A cook ushered me out.

I had no chance to press Nerk for information in the next days, but the incident rekindled my search for Rula's whereabouts, for it meant one could come 'out of the salt' as well as going into it.

Nerk's tasks for me became more numerous and more trivial, sending me frequently to the upper levels of the House. One day, after I had delivered her an inconsequential message about a shortage of capers, the chamberlain laid a hand on my shoulder. She smelled nice, or perhaps only familiar, after so many days of using her old bathwater.

"You had a friend."

Here was an unexpected stroke of luck, and I was not shy to take advantage. "Ma'am. Rula, ma'am. Rula was my friend. She went into the salt." I said the phrase not as I had heard it, with flat fatalism, but with eagerness and optimism. She had gone in, and perhaps she had come out.

The chamberlain looked at me, seemingly more concerned with my demeanour than with my words. I waited expectantly.

"The master will see you," she said.

Until now, the master had been a distant, almost fancied figure in the House, so distant from the concerns of a storesboy that I had never troubled even to imagine him as more than a vague figure in white robes. I stared at the woman, mouth open to protest, except that storesboys did not protest orders from anyone at all, let alone the chamberlain herself.

"Close your mouth. Follow me." She turned, and I followed dumb down hallways of translucent white and pink that grew clearer and finer as we climbed toward the heart of the House. The master himself would tell me about Rula! Perhaps she had caught his eye, become a serving-maid, or even a concubine. Even modest Rula would not turn down such an opportunity, I felt sure.

I barely noted the beauty of the chambers we passed through, the delicate swirls of colour laid by sunshine and salt that we walked through as casually as mirages. I built up my own visions of the welcome Rula would give me, of the warm, tolerant look of the master as he witnessed our reunion, allowed us to hug and hold hands in the warm sanctuary of his presence chamber. As he, why not, served us fresh water with his own hands.

Most of us are fools most of the time. There are many kinds: those who fool themselves, those who are fooled by others, those who are ignorant. All are fools the same, but the most foolish are those who close their eyes and expect the truth to be other than what they see plainly before them.

❦

I spent four years in the salt. Longer than any before me, and still longer than any since. Longer than my kitchen friend, and longer by far than Rula.

The master never called it the salt. He called it the Transcendence. I called it many things, but never that.

The salt is a chamber perfectly cubical, with walls made of the purest, clearest salt blocks, cut so smooth and joined so fine that it is like standing in open air, held up only by an intangible net of faintest white. We trust most what we see, when we bother to see it, but an invisible cage is still a cage.

My prison chamber stood free in the center of the master's parlor near the top of the house, with his study directly below, and the roof walk above. It was furnished with a bed of fine salt crystals, a thick basin of brine, and a privy built of the same clear salt as the walls. Though they had stripped my clothing from me as they lowered me into the chamber from the roof, it was warm enough. I did not notice it, for my attention was taken with tears and pleading.

Ion the fifth day, I tried violence, and it served no better than pleas. Salt, even in purest form, is rock, and rock is stronger than flesh. I soaked my wounds in salt water and cried for pain and shame.

After ten days, I tried to carve my way out with urine, but my urine was already so concentrated as to be little more than a spurt, and so foul-smelling that the smell kept me awake. When my feeble urine-cut in one block grew to a thumb-joint in depth, they replaced the block. I substituted brine from the basin, sprayed from my parched mouth, but it simply pooled on the floor, and the master shut off the flow until the pool had dried into a grey, unhealthy crust.

On all sides of the chamber, at different heights, little holes were bored through the salt, so that he could hear me, and I him. Throughout the day, the master spoke to me.

"Salt, given time and pressure, becomes a rheid. It looks like stone, but it acts like liquid. It transforms itself, transcends its limitations. It can shape itself to fit its surroundings, to escape rigid limits, and become more. More than itself, but without losing its own identity."

He watched me, as he worked, as he slept, as he took his morning walks on the roof above. There was no time that I felt unobserved, free to do the small things we all like to think are private, to pick my nose or scratch my groin. It was no great loss. There had been little privacy among the Bracque, but what Rula found.

He would not speak of Rula, though I asked, demanded, insisted with all my youthful anger.

"You will see her one day," was all he said. "She is waiting for you."

After a month, my spirits were lower than they had been since I first came the salt pit. My fists, torn by battering against crystal walls, stung with every move, every surface they touched. They coated themselves with salt at every bedtime, sluiced it away with every bath. I tried sleeping on the floor, but it was so hard I got no rest. I tried going without bathing, but he stopped providing water – clean water, the water I needed to live.

"You must be clean," he said. "Free of all encumbrance to transcendence."

I fouled the floor, but again he shut off the water, until at last I washed the cell clean. He watched the dirt pour down through the salt pipes, then gave me a small block of coarse gray salt. I scrubbed off layers of floor until only smooth crystal remained and he turned the stopcock and clean water returned.

My joints and muscles hurt for a time, so starved of moisture were they from the constant coating of salt. They had done the same in the salt pit; I had survived there, and I could survive here.

He watched me sleep, eat, cry, piss, shit. He watched my evacuations as they slid slowly down the salt pipes through his bedroom. I thought at first it gave him pleasure, but it did not. It was only data that he noted carefully in his logs.

"It is a question of transparency, you see. Transparency leads to transcendence. That is my hypothesis. It is true of salt, of glass, of water. Why should it not be true of people?"

I laughed in his face. "If I starve myself, I will be so thin you will not see me. Then you will see me transcend for a certainty."

He only shook his head. "Not so, not so. I have seen it tried. Starvation leads only to death. It is not transcendence; far from it." He smiled, stretching the skin across the tight planes of his face. "It is not physical transparency that is important. It is a transparency of the spirit. When your mind is as transparent as this salt, then, you will be closer to transcendence."

I wanted to strike the clear blocks between us, to reach through shattered salt to close my hands around his throat. Yet my hands hurt and I had proven already that the salt was proof against my strength. I tried, instead, to wound him with words.

“I see through you already. Perhaps you will transcend before me. Or die. As you like.” It was little enough, and in fact, I had no real grasp of his purpose, though he had explained it quite sincerely.

“You may be right. We must always acknowledge possibility. However, I lack the second ingredient – not only transparency, but pressure. Salt reforms itself under pressure, and over time. Once we have determined the parameters of pressure and transparency for humans, then you will see me transform indeed, and welcome.”

We were not always alone, the master and I. He had visitors, who attempted to ignore me, and the servants entered whether the master was there or not. They peered at me surreptitiously, as they tidied, stocked, and cleaned, but affected not to see or hear me. Once Nerk climbed up to us, reporting on an infestation of salt-lice in the food-stores. He looked everywhere but towards my cell, even when the master came to stand before me, and I made rude gestures behind his back. Nerk, brave man, only mumbled to the floor, and fled before his report was fairly finished.

“You see,” said the master, when the storesman had gone, “already you begin. You exert your own pressure, beyond the bounds of your small chamber. I'm pleased. It's pressure, remember, that aids the transformation. Enough pressure, and a person will do anything. Most will fracture, like your two friends before you, but some, in just the right circumstances, they will transcend, will become more than they are. I'm sure of it.”

Only the chamberlain seemed to recognize my presence, nodding to me each morning when she arrived for conference with the master over dried fruit and water. Her expression did not change, whether I was clean or covered in filth. She only nodded, sat, and served out the food before listing the day's problems.

Piro came on a regular basis, the slattern who had first greeted me at the House. She was cleaner now, but no more prepossessing. She did her cleaning work quickly, and looked on me with such a mix of relief and fear that I almost pitied her. Instead, I pleaded with her, insulted her, begged her, reviled her. The result was the same; she rushed through her work, leaving streaks of dust across the tables, crumbs of food in the corner. In the end she came no more, replaced by a stolid boy who saw me but made it clear he did not care.

I criticized Piro's work to the master, suggested that a period of transcendence might do her good.

"Oh no," he laughed. "We must start with good material. Piro will never transform. In fact, she has already left the House." He shrugged. "She reached maturity, and the payments stopped." For, as he explained to me, he received payments for support of all children to whom he acted as warden. I grew angrier than before with Piro, who had escaped so easily, but also hopeful, for the news suggested that even this imprisonment must have an end, if only I could survive it. Because I still had not opened my eyes, it took me longer to see the true lesson, which was that Piro had been wiser than me, that the master himself had seen no further than her slovenly garb and mien.

I had hoped to be set free at the four month mark, as the kitchen boy had been. Already, I had forgotten my friend's looks, all memories merging into the same long, angular face, with its perpetual rash along the jaw where salt irritated skin scraped raw by a razor, no matter how gently held.

"It is a travesty," the master called up to me every day as he shaved himself. "But a beard is so hot in this climate, and it catches the salt. Not a worry for you, of course. Not for some time yet."

While I could hardly recall the boy's features, I had held tight to his period of incarceration. Four months. He had held out for four months, and I, who had survived the salt pits, could do no less. But four months went by without change, and then eight.

After a year, the master held a little celebration, he with a carafe of scarlet fruit juice, me with a salt glass of water. As always, I drank it quickly, before it could lose its purity to the salt.

He shook his head. "You must learn to savor these moments. You are, as of today, my best experiment, if not quite a result. It comes of the good raw materials, I believe." He held up his glass to me and sipped. "You have promise, real promise. I think we can go further with you. Already, you begin to see through me." He winked. "That bodes well."

When I asked about release, he tsked and shook his head. "Transcendence," he reminded me gently. "Transcendence is our goal. Do you feel you have transcended?" He shook his head. "Of course not. But you can. I feel it in you. I see it in your skin as it begins to glow." My skin glowed only with a sheen of sweat that streaked the salt away. Beneath, my skin was the same dull beige that it had always been.

After the first year, there was a period of blankness. I ate, I shat, I slept. I stared into nothingness. I thought as little as I was able, and with practice, that was considerable. I believe I went days without a conscious thought, perhaps even weeks or months. I did the minimum to stay alive, to persist, to endure. Yet I have a restless spirit, and even in this condition my mind eventually reawoke.

"You're back," he said, one day, from his desk by the big salt window. And though I had gone nowhere, I laughed. It was true. I had retreated, and found no place to retreat to. In escaping my escape, I found myself back at the start, back in my cell.

"Still hope, then," he added. "Your kitchen friend did the same, much sooner, and I let him go. I see now that it was premature. Or perhaps it's the raw material again."

When I was sure the master still had no intent to let me out, I set to a truly thorough exploration. The walls were more visible to me now, my eyes more accustomed to their faint imperfections, their joins and cracks. But now I searched also with my fingers, aiming to touch every portion of the cell that I could reach. I found uncounted flaws – depressions, chips, rough spots, smooth ones, even, under the bed, deliberate scratches. I passed these over at first, my fingers moving on mechanically before my mind could perform its slow analysis. When I finally awoke to the import of these regular lines, I passed my hands back over them, with a surreptitious glance at the master, who fussed with paperwork under an oil lamp.

R – U – L – A. Rula! I probed eagerly for more, for some message from the past, but this was all. I searched feverishly across the entire underside of the bed, climbing under it entirely, searching with eyes as well as my fingers. I went so far as to lick the entire surface, hoping to catch some sign too faint for hard fingers to discern. There was nothing.

"You've found it, have you?" The master stood outside the wall, watching intently. "I had to teach her the letters. She wasn't as lucky as you in her choice of parents."

I had little enough literacy, and it had not occurred to me that anyone could have less. What did it mean that he had taught her to write her name? I had no doubt that he had. For all his faults, the master never lied to me.

"She was more delicate than you, I'm afraid. It was a lesson for me to look less on the outside than the inside. Your friend didn't know that. She felt the need to leave her mark, and I let her do so."

This physical sign, this direct evidence of Rula's precedence in the salt, heartened me. Rula's mark on the salt was no more than faint scratches, but her trace on me was indelible.

From then on, I did not look back. I lived, I listened, I learned. The master spoke to me of his business, and I saw for myself the meetings he took, the furtive, shadowed figures so uneasy in his transparent house. I took it upon myself to distress them more, noting which looked upon my naked figure with distaste, and which with longing. After a time, the master began discussing their reactions with me.

"Well done. She could hardly keep herself from looking at you, especially when you began to cry, there in the corner. She signed with hardly a look, and I got a far better rate for the prisoners than I dared hope for."

I learned quickly that the master was paid for everything. Money always flowed his way, whether payment for care of prisoners, or for the rock salt they mined, or support payments for the prisoners' children, or for the fine salt they dug in turn. He received payments even for me, and would do so for years, he told me.

"You're my ward, you see? And don't I ward you well?" His laugh was a deep, booming tone that failed to match his lanky frame. "And your friend even better."

When he showed Rula to me, on my two year anniversary in the salt, I was unsurprised. She looked peaceful as he brushed tight-packed salt from her face. Dehydration had stretched her mouth into a rictus that mocked happiness, but her eyes, shrunken and sunk, seemed calm.

"I had to marinate her first, you see? It's important that the salt enter the tissues quickly and thoroughly. She had already opened one artery, of course, and I was able to flush the rest of the blood from the system quickly. The organs were more difficult, and I had to remove the intestines completely. Still, a year in strong brine, and then packed in fine salt, and it's not too bad, is it?"

Her young body looked frail, under its powder of salt, the joints seeming swollen on withered limbs. Across her ribs, an extra pair of tiny limbs dangled loose, one arm, one leg, like a child climbing slowly out or in above the devastation of her belly.

"Interesting, aren't they? You get that, sometimes, especially in some regions. It's the result of one twin eating the other, I believe, but not finishing the job. Your friend was quite sensitive about it."

I imagined hard, proud, private Rula, exposed here for the master's observation, imagined her sitting in one corner or another, trying without success to hide her secret, the secret she had kept from me and from the Bracque, even there in the closeness of the salt pit. I pictured her succumbing to despair at last, forced to turn to her tormentor to ask even for the means to leave a mark, a sign of her own sad existence.

The salt had changed me as well, left me with a surface hard and sleek and impervious. I polished away my tears before they could disturb the glaze of my exterior, mar me and show the master more than a pale reflection of his self. I asked about preservation techniques, and about the uses of salt, and about transformation.

"Oh, you're getting on, you are. You'd make a fine assistant, if I did not have other uses for you." Yet the skin flushed dark across his rash, and I could tell that for all his easy way, he was disturbed by the failure of his scheme.

He seemed to lose heart when even the sight of Rula failed to make me transform. He turned his attention briefly to other, more extreme means.

"We must work with the materials at hand, after all, and salt is what we have in plenty. Salt not only transforms itself, but is transformative of others, can we only find how to apply it." His attempts were grotesque, and there were days I felt happier inside my salt chamber than without. More and more of the servants found ways to leave the House, whether at maturity or not. The Bracque brought some back, but not many. Even the Bracque have their limits, and they made clear they found the master's work distasteful. After a time, he gave it up, though he kept Rula on display for me next to my chamber, and I watched as her flesh slowly shrank, and a faint pink slurry formed at the bottom of her box, until at last she seemed to float above a slab of marble.

It was two more years before I convinced the master that he had failed, that my value as secretary was more than the slim chance of my transformation to invisible super-man. I spent the years in careful study, learning to read and write and count properly, so that I could record my own data for him. I continued to distress his visitors, and memorized his intricate web of transactions so that I could advise him and remind him. He placed visitors with their back to my cage, and we devised a simple system of signs that I could give surreptitiously, behind their backs. At times they gave themselves away to me with a mumble while he posed against the far window.

I planned my replacement for him. He had started his experiments with the young, more an artistic choice than a scientific one. I argued that the subject needed more more complex, more experienced material in order to transform. He had his doubts, but once Nerk was installed in my place, he nodded grudgingly.

“I never chose you, boy,” the old man cried. “Don't do this. Don't you think I paid the price for you in my heart, all the time you've been in here? And the girl before you? And the others?”

“What was her name, Nerk?” I asked. Turning my head, I said “You see, master, there's an emotional component from which a younger subject simply does not benefit.”

“I don't know, boy, any more than I know yours. There are so many... And I'm an old man. But I cared. I really cared.” Nerk's eyes were hopeless, and I turned my back.

The master nodded. "There's something in what you say. When you came in, you didn't show the same sense of betrayal, quite."

"A child knows little of such things. It takes age to experience betrayal fully."

At our backs, Nerk subsided into a tangle of bones and belly as we retreated to the relative silence of the window.

"You may be right. I grant you that it generates more pressure, and pressure is what's needed, if my hypothesis is correct."

"Of course it is, master. But now we must focus on expanding the salt markets to the south-east." We turned to other matters.

Once I was out of the salt, I needed little enough time to do my task. I took on more and more of the trivial, ministerial chores, and the correspondence, and finally the meetings themselves.

Now, he smiles up at me as the work goes on around us.

"I should have seen this coming," he admits.

I nod. "You neglected the effect of diffraction. At the proper angle, a thing can be seen even around a corner."

He cocks his head to one side. "Interesting indeed. But what effect would it have on my theory of transformation, do you think?"

I smile. "We shall see, master. We shall see." I step back to allow the workmen to set another block between us. "I've taken the liberty of increasing the pressure to account for it." On the floor below us, workmen remove the salt piping that ran through the master's bedroom, and they spray the new plug with brine that will crystallize in the interestices and act as mortar. “I expect careful records, mind.”

“Of course.” They seal the final block in place, leaving us to ourselves.

After a time, the visitors that do enter the House are again disappointed. The salt room has become repellent, I fear. The master has not maintained his focus on cleanliness, and he weeps dreadfully much of the time. I have faith, though, that he will transcend, that some day I will wake and look through my ceiling to find him gone. In her box beside my bed, Rula waits patiently to celebrate.

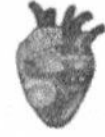

About the story

I'm a big fan of Richard Llewellyn's *How Green Was My Valley*. He may not have been very Welsh, but for me as a young boy, he absolutely captured the feel of a place I could see and hear. I'd been thinking about the book and its unique voice, and wanted to try something along those lines myself. The plot, of course, is very distant from those green hills and piles of slag, but I was pretty happy with the voice of the piece. The piece is far closer to horror than what I usually write, but I like it.

Full of Stars

The jar had held pickles, once. Now, it was full of stars. She'd soaked the label off, then buffed the inside and outside until, at the right angle, it looked like the lid was just floating on air. Aside from the stars.

"Mom, Oni's got fireflies," said her brother. "Make her let them out!" But they came and saw nothing, and went away muttering hopeful words like "imagination" and "savant".

"Whatcha got in there, weirdo?" giggled Yakini, the playground bully. "Invisible fairies?" She and her cronies fell down laughing, laughing, at the girl with the empty jar.

After school, she lay in the shadowed house with the jar by her bed, letting the light of the stars play across her face. "Capella," she said, pointing at her favorite. "Algol," she named another as it swept past in its swirling dance.

At night, with the village asleep but the dogs awake, she crept out to the commons. She lay back against hard, dusty ground, and sought out a thinly-populated stretch of sky just down from Cassiopeia. With a smile on her lips, and a pickle jar held close to her heart, she willed one more star into being.

About the story

This is one of a very few stories I've written to send to a particular market. I generally don't write flash, but AE had announced a call for microstories. I wasn't writing much at the time and I thought that a microstory sounded like just about what I had time to do. I believe the stories were required to deal with stars, and the image of a jar full of stars just came to me. It wasn't until later that I realized I'd echoed a line from *2001*.

Memory and Faded Ink

She liked to watch me sleeping. “I always remember you like this,” she would say. “Drowsing in a pool of sunlight, dawn pouring off you like gold. That is how I know you are rich.”

When she was young, rich to Tseleng was time enough to weed millet, and light enough to spot vipers. To me, it meant a roof that didn’t leak. When the Buyani arrived, it meant them, and suddenly the whole planet was poor.

They were generous enough; the very definition of philanthropists — they loved humans. They even said they were human themselves, and they looked the part — tall and strong, with tight copper curls, aquiline features, loamy skin. If ever our gods come back, they will look like this. The Buyani were as human as aliens could be. Too human.

They weren’t really Buyani, of course, any more than they were Atlanteans, or Lemurians, or Muans, or any other lost race. They admitted that their vast ship could land, could submerge, but they left it at the L1 Lagrange point, between the sun and an Earth turned upside down by surprise and suspicion, by alien wizards and wonders.

In those drowsy, golden mornings, we'd talked about it, Tseleng and I, and in the busy afternoons, when she sold her books with Mamekete and Leabua, the weathered sages of Maseru's open air market.

"They say alphabets are for children," Tseleng would tell us. "They say letters are the stick figure art of communication — a primitive tool to be left behind along with counting on fingers and uncertain bladder control."

"No one will buy books anymore," Leabua would say, wiping dust off his piles of outdated textbooks and social science tracts.

"No one buys them now," Mamekete would reply, determined to match pessimism with cynicism at every turn. But she would wipe her own stock of novels and poetry chapbooks nonetheless.

"The Buyani don't have any books. Do you really think they remember everything?" Tseleng would say, playing optimist. "People say they even have some sort of racial memory."

"Too much information," I would say. "Where could they store it all?" Every group needs a sceptic, and Serbs are naturals at it.

"It's just transmitters in their brains," Leabua would say. "The information's in the cloud." And then the conversation would circle back to whether the Buyani were really human, and whether they had left us behind, or visited before, and whether their other ships were shaped like islands or pyramids or mountains.

The Buyani wouldn't say. They were chary with information about themselves, but they gave technology freely, so that even in Lesotho, we had free energy, and clean water, and synthesized food.

"It's a trick," I told Tseleng one day, as she smoked pot under a black locust tree. "They'll make us all dependent on them, and then," I made a fist, "they'll have us."

"They have us now." They'd shown no signs of violence, but no one made any pretense that we could win a war. A few hotheads, a few suicide bombers, a few terrorists had tried, but with the Buyani present, bullets floated to a gentle stop, bombs set off slow, soft breezes, and toxins faded into nothingness. There were still wars, of course, but they were small, local scuffles over religion and other trivia. Life, even for sceptics, was better.

I gave this to the Buyani — their distribution network was efficient. Even on the dirt roads outside Maseru, we got their latest gifts as soon as anyone on the boulevards of Boston, or the cobblestones of Quito.

Those lazy conversations would have been the sum of it, should have been the total of my experience of the Buyani. Until they came to us, and Tseleng went to them.

We all have our means of escape. For me, it was travel. Outside the grim, stuffy confines of Belgrade, with its cheery sidewalk cafes overflowing with dour traditionalists, its bright, modern shops selling things no one could afford. I'd gone south, to Greece, and Egypt, and Rwanda, and South Africa, and finally Lesotho. Tseleng had escaped with drugs. From glue bottles on the paths of her nameless village to harder fare on the roads of Maseru.

We'd met halfway, each deciding to try something new. For her, a tall, exotic foreigner, for me, a joint or two in a shabby bar. And it had worked. I'd settled down, she'd let the hard stuff drift away. It hadn't been easy, not for either of us. But it had been worth it.

And then the Buyani came. Only a dozen years after that huge ship appeared, and the radio told us all that life had changed, they came to Lesotho.

"What do they want?" I'd asked her, when she came home one day, still flustered after an encounter in the market. "Why would they come here?" We only ever like the changes we make ourselves, and sometimes not even those.

"They seek the pure people," she'd said. "They want excitement. They are young, these Buyani who have come to us."

Too young. Too exciting. And nowhere near pure enough.

"They speak perfect Sesotho," she'd said. "I told them we were as pure as you could want. Up here in the mountains, in our isolation, you could not ask for more purity. We do not mix with others."

Unless you counted South Africans, or itinerant Serbs like me. But she was happy, and that was worth any number of sharp comebacks. I wish I'd learned that earlier.

"You should meet them," she'd said. "You can be giants together."

They were giant enough, and good looking enough, to make me jealous. I was human enough to try to hide it.

“I’m busy,” I told her, and so we spent our days apart, and some of our nights, too.

“I’ll take them to my village,” she said, and I nodded in false confidence, because why wouldn’t sophisticated aliens be interested in a nameless agglomeration of clay huts and tin roofs?

“It’s very pure,” I said with a little bite, because no matter how we pretend, we’re all limbic lizards at the core.

Tseleng’s lizard was less active than most, and she’d just shrugged and taken three giant aliens on a week-long road trip. I was sorry by the time she got back, and she’d forgotten all about it.

“Your Buyani friends wouldn’t have,” I pointed out, as if it were a winning point, as if bringing them down to my level of pettiness would make them less attractive, and me more so.

“Their memories are their pride,” she said, and kissed me. “I am hoping they will teach that trick to me.” I remembered that later, as I looked around our little mokhoro, with its concrete floor and mud walls and absence of Tseleng.

I woke early, and alone. “It’s their last night in Maseru,” she’d told me. “They want to celebrate.” I had thought she might be late, or drunk, or both. But now, as the dawn light ran down the tin of the roof and the stone of the walls, I wondered whether I should have expected her at all. The bed beside me was empty, untouched by anything but my own midnight thrashing. There was no sign Tseleng had been there, and deep in my gut, the lizard shook its tail and spat.

I ate old, dry toast, eschewing the flavored nutrient blocks of the Buyani synthesizer, dipped water from our old, stale well in place of clear, safe water pulled like magic from the air. It was childish, and I knew it, but sometimes the smallest acts of resistance are all you have.

I dawdled through my shower, my resolve too weak to forgo solar-heated comfort in favor of mere principle. But when I emerged, to towel dry under a warm November sun, Tseleng was still not back, and at last I accepted the inevitable. If she would not come back to me, I would go to her, Buyani or no.

I passed through the market, first, through the jumble of rusting tools to the heaps of vegetables with their flies. In the tea stalls, I found Mamekete.

"Lumelang, 'me-Mamekete," I said.

"Good morning to you as well, young one." She looked troubled.

"Have you seen Tseleng?"

"I... In the market. I think." She looked like she wanted to add more, but she and Leabua can talk for hours, once they're started.

"Leboha, 'me." I left her there, no doubt deploring the awfulness of my Sesotho, and commiserating with the tea sellers about outlanders.

Tseleng was back! Not to our home, no, but to work in the market, and that could only mean the Buyani were gone. I had a bounce in my step and a smile on my lips as I wended my way through the stalls to the quiet area where books were, if not sold, at least displayed.

"Lumelang, ntate Leabua," I offered with my best accent as I passed the old man by. I ignored his gestures, my eyes intent on the spare form of a short woman at a neighbouring table.

"Tseleng!" I leaned across the table to kiss her. "I missed you."

She smiled back at me, bemused. "Well," she said, "perhaps I have missed you too."

"No perhaps about it," I shook my head, though I'd expected a little more enthusiasm. "You have missed me like corn misses rain, like potatoes miss rosemary, like stars miss the night." But she didn't smile her 'I love you for your foolishness' smile.

"I will take you at your word," she said, and ran her eyes over my t-shirt and my jeans. "You seem a likely enough fellow. Come and smoke with me."

"What?" I'd only smoked with her that one time. It had made me sick, and since then she'd known to stand downwind of me when she lit up.

"Just some cannabis," she assured me. "Nothing strange. A little nausea won't hurt you."

"I don't ..." I looked into her eyes, and they were playful, warm. Everything but loving. "Tseleng, what's wrong? What have they done to you?"

She winked. "Did you know that even the Buyani have drugs? Of course they do. Everyone has drugs."

"What do you mean? What did they give you?" This was not Tseleng. Or, at least, it was, but not the Tseleng I'd lived with for the past three years. The one I'd bonded with, loved with, grown with, planned with.

"I took a Buyani drug, once," she said, undeterred by my growing anger. "They said it works on memory." She giggled. "I remember them saying that. Like Russian roulette for memory, they said. Big trouble if they get caught."

A chill ran through my heart. A new drug, a Buyani drug, a memory drug. And of course she had taken it.

"Where are they?" I took her by the arm, shook her. "Tseleng, where are they?" I would find them, threaten them, beat them, whatever it took to find out what had happened.

"There's no point," said a sad voice behind me. It was Leabua, come shuffling out from behind his table. "They're gone. They drove out last night, apparently. I spoke with the hotel."

"What happened?" I tried to keep calm, to keep from shaking this old, frail man, with his old, irrelevant books, and their tired, faded ink no one would ever read.

"What you know. They played some game, took pills. Mostly they enhance memory. One pill in a thousand erases it. Tseleng lost."

"What? But... why?"

"Why does anyone? For excitement, for escape. For the chance of freedom."

"And Tseleng?" What freedom had she sought?

He shrugged, his eyes wet. "She lost. Lost her memory. Not all of it. She knows who she is, who we are. It's the associations that are gone, the links. She knows I'm Leabua, that Mamekete is Mamekete." Mamekete had come up now, had joined our little circle in silent commiseration.

"She knows she has known us, has loved us," Mamekete said. "She doesn't now." She seemed tired, even the cynicism in her beaten down by cruel reality. "Whatever formed that link between past and present is missing." She looked at me sadly. "She knows you, too. Or knows she knew you."

"And doesn't care?" It seemed bizarre, outlandish. As, of course, it was.

"And doesn't care," confirmed Leabua. "No more than she cares about us." As if that mattered to me.

I spent hours with her, that day and night, discovering only that they had told the truth. Tseleng came home with me, knew it for her home as well. She made love to me, and it was good, as if it were something new and exciting and different. Through it all, she treated me as a stranger, a fun discovery, with no more history than a new-bloomed flower. In the morning, she said goodbye as if I were some one-night stand.

We called in the authorities, the police, the diplomats. It was an international scandal. And if anything confirmed the essential humanity of the Buyani, it was this, that their young behaved just as foolishly as ours. For all their high technology, their vaunted memory, they took the same stupid risks, made the same unwise choices, paid the same costly prices.

The Buyani found our visitors quickly. They gave them a variant of the same drug Tseleng had taken. "They'll lose their memories," they said. "They'll be like new people." To Buyani, it was the ultimate punishment. To me, it was nothing at all. Once I found Tseleng's loss could not be remedied, I stopped talking with them.

"This is a terrible crime," their Ambassador told me at our last meeting. He frowned his god-like frown, ran strong fingers through curly hair, let a tear run across his perfect face. "We will do anything we can to make it right, give you anything you ask."

"Can you give me back Tseleng?" I asked. He didn't answer, and I left.

Tseleng still sells her pamphlets and brochures in the market place. I buy one from time to time, or read her some of Pheko Motaung's poetry in my atrocious Sesotho. We still live together. We're friends, I'd say. Maybe good friends. But we're different people.

When I came in from my shower this morning, she was still lying in bed, with the sun just peeking over the windowsill.

"I remember you like this," she said. "Lying in bed, wasting good sunlight. It is how I know you were rich." I smiled and kissed her on the cheek before starting breakfast. I was rich, once. Someday, with a little patience, I will be again.

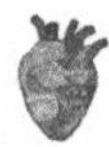

About the story

I don't recall the genesis of the idea, but I know that the seed of the story was the idea of loss of memory as a punishment. The Buyani developed as an exemplar of culture built on memory that would be particularly affected. My disaffected protagonist pretty quickly grew jealous of aliens who are effortlessly better at everything, despite the fact that he hasn't even been trying. I set the story in Lesotho as a nod to a relative who spent a lot of time there, with a tip of the hat to some of the development types I've met in my own overseas ventures.

Fountainhead

"I'm sorry," she said at last. She had been staring out the window – a 'phore', they called it here – watching starbirds hover in their pastel stacks, like floating towers of origami. She wondered how they did it, and whether she it might be what she needed for her 'Fountain' piece. Or maybe 'Fountainpiece'.

She turned back to the delegation, to find they hadn't moved at all. Their fingers fluttered over gleanberry juice and cinnakick, but their faces wore the same uncomprehending puzzlement they'd shown the first time she said it.

"I'm sorry," she said again, though repetition didn't seem to help. "I can't do it. I *won't* do it. I don't want it."

Keleba, the composer, and hence leader of the delegation, put on the same smile she'd tried before. "Perhaps, Livia, we've not been quite clear." The other two nodded affirmingly, if without conviction. "This is a signal honor. A unique opportunity to exponentially improve your art. A ... " It seemed she had run out, finally, of superlatives.

"I know," Livia said, to fill the gap. She looked each of them confidently in the eye, the way Kipo had always said to do when negotiating a sale. She looked out the window again – the *phore.* Kipo would never have been in this situation to begin with. And without Kipo, neither would she. "I know how special the offer is. How unique a moment it is for me – and the other 2,000 artists on Glir." Taciturn Melen raised an eyebrow, but the others didn't seem to hear the acerbity in her tone. "But I don't want it."

"You misunderstand, Livia," and now it was clear that Keleba had caught her tone just fine. "It's not a matter of choice. If you want to stay on Glir, you *must* accept a muse. You will take one," she said, stroking the fuzzy creature wrapped around her own shoulder, "or you will leave the planet. Those are the rules."

"There's a freighter outbound from the orbital in three days," chimed in Meva at last, hes muse's long soft legs wrapped around hes head in a parody of a hat. "And a shuttle up in two. Decide by then. Or leave."

They'd been readier than she thought, she admitted as she cleared the dishes and put them in the cleaner. They'd been polite as long as they could stand it, but in the end the claws had come out. Kibo had probably warned them, let them know Livia was a difficult character. *You're too caught up the whole artistic mystique,* Kibo had said, when they parted ways at last. *It keeps you from seeing the truth. That's why your art is so ...* Se'd left the phrase unfinished, but not the thought. *Pedestrian,*

Livia knew se meant. *Trite.* Se'd never had to say it outright. *Unsaleable.* Kibo was a master of implication, of possibility. People across the galaxy paid double for pieces se abandoned partway through. Se finished most of them anyway.

Just as se'd finished with Livia. Out of principle. *I need to explore new horizons,* se'd said. *And now who's being trite?* Livia had asked. And that had been it. Kibo had been gone the next day, leaving all hes unfinished pieces behind, all carefully signed and listed. Millions of sols worth of goodbye note. And a heart that would never be complete again.

She couldn't leave. Not with Kibo still on Glir, albeit halfway across the planet. Not with a chance, however slim that they could be together again. *You have no pride,* Kibo had said about one of her pieces once, a pencil sketch of a leaf with a little frog-like creature just peeking out from under. And she didn't. She'd loved that sketch, even if it was boring and derivative and schmaltzy. She'd framed it and put in her study. And she'd go flying back to Kibo in a heartbeat if she could. There was no helping it. Even Kibo admitted it. 'The Strong Force', se'd called the piece that had won hem the Spiral award – an array of magnets that flew apart if nudged just right, but always flew right back together again. *It's a love poem,* se'd said in hes acceptance vid, and se'd smiled at Livia as se said it. And now they both were gone.

She slept surprisingly well that night, even coming up with a new angle for the 'Fountainpiece', a way to work in the starbirds, so that the flowers around the little spring at the center curled up into birds that spiraled up into the trees above. It wasn't genius, but she was happy with it, and it kept her busy all that day, and most of the night.

The next day, she slept as late as she could, as if by ignoring the matter, she could put it off indefinitely. But the truth was her decision was made, had been made as soon as Keleba and her delegation left. She couldn't leave. And if that meant sacrificing her pride, her artistic core, well, she'd prepare the altar herself.

"I'll stay," she told the delegation when they came in the afternoon. And, when Melen's eyebrow spoke for him again, she made it clear. "I'll take a muse."

"Well," said Keleba quietly. "That is good news." But she'd caught them by surprise, she could tell. They'd brought no muse with them, aside from their own, those fuzzy, colour-patterned snake-spiders that were Glir's primary value to the rest of the galaxy. "You won't regret it. I wrote music before I was awarded a muse," – Keleba had won the Spiral herself when she was barely thirty – "but until I got this one," she stroked the thing, now on her right shoulder, "I didn't *compose*." And it was true that Keleba's work had improved exponentially once she came to Glir. Livia herself thought so. What had been brilliant was now sublime. But was it her music, or the muse's, or some awful hybrid?

"I'll talk with the Council," Melen said. The Council of Glirbesan, he meant – the assortment of humans and aliens who ruled Glir as an arts foundation, and who parceled out muses accordingly. "They were never happy with your ...

unusual situation." The fact that they'd wanted Kibo so much that they'd broken precedent to allow hem to bring along hes museless lover. "They'll be glad to have it regularized." Though Livia could sense Kibo's hand even in this offer.

Livia looked out the phore again. There had been a leaf-fall again last night, the third this week, and the lawn was littered with them. Each with a little frog-thing hidden under it, more than likely. *Frigs,* Kibo called them, *because they're all over the frigging place.*

"They'll probably have one for you in a week," offered Meva to fill the silence. "They have to find just the right one," leaving Livia confused about frigs and muses and falling leaves.

They knew the right one apparently, by her interaction with Glir. *It's not a world mind,* Kibo had said, when they arrived, *but there's sort of communal record ... or spirit, or trace, or something, that we leave behind. They use it to find the muse that's the best fit to your needs. And it's a great honor for the muses as well, apparently,* she'd said, forestalling a caustic comment. *They don't create. But they enhance. That's what they dream of, it's said – participating in art.*

Not all of them, apparently. They'd introduced her to her muse in a drab, pre-built hut, shabby from a generation of use. The muse was a shocking electric blue, with a kind of plaid pattern of grey lines that spiraled around its eight legs – tentacles? – and faded away in the mud-green scaly patch that seemed to count as its head.

"It will tell you it's name," Meva said. "Or ... well, not a name, exactly. But you'll ... you'll just know what you mean when you call it. And so will it, and it will come."

Only, this one didn't come. And when Meva called it over, it flatted like a starfish, like it was gripping the little table with every tentacle. They couldn't pick it up. Livia had even tried stroking it with a finger, just to get it over with. It felt nice, like a plush toy, and it smelled, disconcertingly, of aniseed. But it had only flattened even more, as if to pull away from her touch.

At last, Meva's own muse, a brownish checked thing that moved with the fluid grace of a squid, had swirled over and sat on it, slowly wrapping brown tentacles around blue until they were braided into ever-tightening cords, and Livia was afraid one of them would burst. Then Meva's had suddenly let go and danced back to Meva.

The blue one had swooshed up, then, so that it stood tall on delicate legs, and minced slowly, reluctantly, she thought, over to wrap itself around Livia's forearm.

It was a moment of magic. She knew the muse, all of a sudden. Knew that it was ... who it was and what it was, and that she could call it Bluid for short. Knew as well that it was no more pleased with the arrangement than she, and that not all muses longed to help gangly, ugly aliens with dull brown skin do whatever they did, when they could be husbanding a beautiful patch of scrubland that was just recovering from some other alien's excavations for raw material. And she knew that Bluid knew her just as well. *No hard feelings,* she told it, and knew that it disliked her bony, squishy arm as much as she disliked its fuzzy, corded tentacles.

"There!" said Meva happily. "I'm sure you'll be great friends," she said with a little too much hope, and scurried away.

You can get off now, Livia thought, and immediately knew that it couldn't. That *they* would know, and that *they* was the other muses. That if they know Bluid wasn't doing its part, they would shun it, and for a muse, she somehow knew, shunning was death.

But why? she asked, and knew that she would never understand, that it was some mix of humor and propriety and duty – too alien to grasp, but nonetheless certain for that.

Then let's get out of this awful hut. And with that, at least, Bluid agreed.

They established, early on, that Bluid must spend most of its time in contact with her. That if it didn't, it would die, and that if it died, she would have to leave, and that would be the end of her and Kibo, if there was ever to be a them again.

She learned that she didn't need to talk to it, that they understood each other wordlessly, and instantly. She did it anyway, in an internal monologue that didn't seem to make things worse, at least. *And it makes things easier for me.* Though it knew her thoughts well before she finished verbalizing them.

They moved, as well. *If we're to be each other's slaves*, she told it, *at least let it be in familiar surroundings.* She moved her house, such as it was, to Bluid's piece of scrubland, so that they could keep an eye on its development. *And a more desolate piece of waste ground I've never seen.* Whatever alien had taken its materials here had left a mostly barren scree of gravel, with a sickly bush here or there, and a litter of potholes to make the walking hazardous. No trees, no starbirds. Not even any frigging frigs.

She put up an instapod, an ugly little cube with all the modern conveniences, and room for one, plus a little studio. She'd tried to leave Kibo's works to their fate, as some kind of statement of independence. In the end, though, she'd boxed them up and left them safely stored in the bolewood they'd live in together, with its window-phores and soft, punky walls, and rough-bark root steps down to the lawn.

She packed and stored and moved and built and settled. And then she sat at her easel, and looked out at the gravel and she cried. For herself, for losing Kibo, for selling her creativity in this devil's bargain, with a devil that didn't even want to be bound. She cried for Bluid's ruined scrubland, for what it could have been, for the evil that humans brought with them wherever they went. Though it wasn't just humans, of course, but all the other aliens on Glir as well. And mostly it wasn't evil at all.

It is for me, she said, sobbing. And that was true as well. *And for you.* And so it was. She saw it clearly, as clearly as she'd ever seen anything, and she saw that there was beauty in that evil as well, or at least art. *There's art in everything,* Kibo had said, soon after they'd arrived. And now she know what se had meant.

She saw, with the awful clarity Bluid offered, that 'Fountainpiece' was slight and obvious and, worst of all, false, and that the best thing she could do with it was abandon it. And she refused.

Bluid backed her fully. It had stayed on her forearm at first, but it got in the way, and eventually they had settled on her calf as a better spot. Just as 'distant' feeling, but less trouble. It did its best to withdraw its consciousness from her, and she from it, but neither had much success. Their effect on each other was natural and ineluctable. Though it made them both unhappy, it was a fact that the effect itself made clear.

She worked on 'Fountainpiece', staying as close to her original vision as she could, though she could not help but smooth away some of the flaws, making the starbirds less of a transformation, and more an emergence. Which was what they did anyway, she now knew – they laid their eggs, for want of a better term, in the thick stems of the purple flowers, and when they grew enough to split those open, they unfurled their five wings and crawled up into the trees. They tethered themselves to branches like spiders, she realized, and spiraled down and reeled back up until the wind brought them within reach of another branch. They weren't floating stacks at all, but birds tangling threads as part of their mating dance.

It's always disappointing to see the trick behind the magic, she said, but she saw the beauty of it, the more complex reality, and she painted that into her piece.

It wasn't genius. It never would be, starting as it had from a false premise. But it was heartbreaking nonetheless, and the best work she'd ever done. She signed it, and packed it up and sent it to Kibo, where se was living in the mountains with two men.

'Good', said Kibo's note, and that was all, but she stroked the notepaper, and smelled it, and cried over it nonetheless. And then she set to work, not with brush and pencil, but with rake and bucket.

She had thought, at first, that she would replant, bring green and red and purple to sit amid the gravel, and gentle it, heal it. Not exactly an apology to Bluid, for neither of them had chosen this unhappy pairing, but a thanks. She knew that she could not have painted the true 'Fountainpiece' without it, and that the old her would have seen the brilliance of it, would have recognized it as the masterwork it was. She hadn't lost herself in the partnership. Not yet, at least.

She laid out her tools, her shovel and hoe, and then set them aside. Instead, at Bluid's urging, she sat and she watched, and she lay and she felt. In the sun, the night, the rain, the heat. And gradually, she saw what it saw. That the ruin of the land was not the broken stone and jagged gravel, the sere grass and stunted bushes, but the small nest of crawlers that was eating its winter food supplies, because a slab was blocking their exit, and they couldn't tunnel out. The delicate floret that was covered in rockdust and not getting the sun it needed to trigger its pheromones. The rill that ran clear instead of pooling murky and foul and full of nutrients for the worms that emerged only once in a year to eat. So, slowly, carefully, she raked and she dug with her hands, and move rocks with a prybar, but only once she was certain. And when they had done what they could, she cried again, because Bluid was happy – as happy as a slave could be – and because with Livia's bigger, stronger body, they done more than it could have by itself.

They moved, then, to another wasteland, and another, and another. Until it had been years, and Kibo had written to say that 'Fountainpiece' had won the Spiral award, and shouldn't she paint again?

And so, for hem, she did. By then, the muses had allowed Bluid some freedom, and they ranged free of each other, within limits. They slept together, but spent their days apart, still linked, and never more than a dozen meters apart, but no longer touching.

Bluid like to slither across the land, learning it and its inhabitants – where they should be, how they'd been harmed, how they could be helped. That was the muses' niche, she knew now. Their instincts, their empathy were a tool the land used to heal itself after earthquakes, lightning strikes, wildfires. Not in some vague, earthmothery way, but in a very practical sense. This was Glirian civilization, she realized. Directed not at mastering nature, but rebuilding it, making it the best it could be. Not the best for the muses, she saw, but the best for the planet.

That was the secret of the muses – that their purpose was to make others the best they could be. That, to a muse, was true development. And Bluid, she realized, was a master in its own right – a talented, well-respected genius of accompaniment and potential.

No wonder you hate being stuck with me, she said wryly, and there was no false modesty to it. They both knew it was true, and that she too would have preferred to create art on her own terms. *I need to do it by myself,* she said, *even if it's not as* good. And that was true too. And she laughed, because Bluid, in its own way, told her its first joke, by somehow showing her a truth about herself – that mating dance of the frig was to hide under the smallest leaf it could shoulder under and still be largely unseen – and that a hidden frig was a proud frig.

She painted only two more pieces. She drew a pencil study of a frig under a tiny leaf that failed to hide a pride as large and bright as a star. She titled it 'Electromagnetism', and sent it to Kibo, and it won the Spiral as well – the only time an artist had ever won it twice.

The second piece was a study of a blue plaid muse wrapped around a rotten piece of wood. She hung that in her instapod, and cried over it after Bluid reached its final maturity and split into mindless budlings.

When at last Kibo came to her and urged her to get another muse and to paint more and to come back and live with hem, she hugged hem and cried again, and said no. *This is my easel,* she said to herself, and dug her hands into a bog that someone had filled in with dirt, *and these are my brushes.*

When Kibo left, she thought longingly of what might have been and should have been, and she watched Bluid's budlings crawling through the mud, and lay down next to them to try to learn what they most needed.

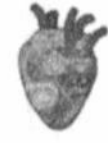

About the story

I don't usually participate in my own anthologies, but with *Score*, I thought I'd give it a shot. The first story had promise, but I just couldn't get it to work right. This second one went better, and took a stab at a third with "The Humblebract Expedition". When it turned out I had two slots to fill, I used the latter two. This one was meant to convey sorrow and longing.

Probably based on something that came up in my work, I started with the idea of forced marriage, and the idea that the community thinks both sides should be happy with the result, but of course neither is.

I began with a woman who's been left — for no good reason — by her much more famous partner. In an indication of how poorly they understand each other, the leaver arranges an alien 'honor' for her ex — the 'forced marriage'. Except that neither the ex nor the alien feels very honored by it. I wanted to depart from the typical 'enemies become friends' trope by having the two learn to get along, but still not give up on the fact that they'd have preferred to be alone.

Adaptations to Coastal Erosion

It was after summer that Nora started to sink. Just footsteps a little deeper than usual; she saw them as she came back on her walk, comparing her outgoing, energetic pace to her homecoming, philosophical one. The prints were firm and well defined in the hard wet sand, but *deep*, and she tried to remember whether she had been running. But the toeprints were too clean, and besides, running, at her age? Examined, her memory yielded only sand dollars, seagulls, and seals. For a sand dollar, one stooped, for a seal, one stopped. One might run for seagulls, she supposed, or a dog might.

The footprints were deeper than normal; that was the main thing. Something to tell Elsie, to cheer her up. Nora felt she wasn't constitutionally suited to heaviness, but for Elsie – Elsie, who battled her weight constantly and vocally – she would give it her best shot.

She didn't feel the weight as she walked home. Down at the shoreline, the sand was firm and smooth and wet beneath her feet, just as it should be. There was less sand these days. The rip-rap that protected houses made the sand wash away. But there was still plenty, and it still felt like sand. It felt nice between her toes. She might even walk further tomorrow – up to the north end of the village, perhaps. "I wish you wouldn't go so far," Elsie always said. "Maybe I should go with you." But Elsie's didn't care for long walks. "You stay here," Nora always said. "Have a good healthy lunch waiting when I get back. I'll be hungry!" And Elsie would whip out her cookbooks and sit for an hour happily planning out an elaborate lunch that always required more ingredients than they had on hand. "I'll go into town," she'd say, and then be frazzled about getting it all done in time and still having time to paint in the afternoon.

When Nora got back to her starting point, she stopped to rest and watch a chain of pelicans fly by. There would be more tomorrow; there were always seals, and gulls, and pelicans, and eagles on the Oregon coast. Cells of the world mind, carrying thoughts from place to place. She smiled at what Elsie would say to such wooly thinking. She'd probably claim sarcastically that the pelicans were just agents of the Thunderbird. Perhaps they were. According to Elsie's Tillamook tribe, this was the age of 'true happenings'. Perhaps it was pelicans that brought them.

She turned inland, climbing the giant steps laid in the stone rip-rap. She and Elsie sat at the top sometimes, in the afternoon, Elsie painting, Nora reading or napping. She moved slowly now, mindful of her balance. Rock was hard, and bone was brittle – especially old bone.

The mid-morning sun shone soft and warm on her cheek as she reached the top. Down at the end of the street, she could see their open front door. No doubt Elsie would pop out any minute now, worried about the three pans on the little stove, the sheet of something sweet baking in the oven. The house was a tiny shoebox of a thing, with sitting room, kitchen, bathroom, and bedroom laid out in a narrow shotgun format. The kitchen was too small for them to share cooking duties, but it was Elsie's domain anyway, just as the beach was Nora's.

A wide form swayed through the door, and Nora waved. Too far to call out, but Elsie just nodded and rushed back in. She'd be desperate to get everything ready in time, just as a moment ago she'd have despaired of it drying out. It would be perfect, as it always was.

"Honey, I'm home," Nora called when she reached the porch. She sat to brush crusted sand off her feet and exchange sandals for slippers. "I'm hungry. And I'm fat, too."

Fat! That would be the day, thought Elsie. Nora was like a seagull – all hollow bones and fluff. She ate, though. A lot, when you came right down to it. Elsie lived vicariously through Nora's desserts. Cinnamon rolls today; she could smell the sweet, rich dough with dark brown sugar and a hint of cloves mixed in. Delicious. You had to taste each batch to be sure they came out right, and these had; just right.

"Stop mocking me and lay the table," she told Nora. Her lover looked the same as always – a wiry frame of pale, freckled skin with smears of sunblock on the back of her neck. If she'd had an ounce of fat, you'd see it.

"No, really," Nora called, going back to the front room, where the table was already laid. "My footprints were deeper."

"Deeper than what?" Elsie brought out plates loaded with tofu scramble, sautéed asparagus, and mashed potatoes. If she squinted at the dish, it was a nice abstract, but abstracts didn't sell. "Did they say something profound to you?" You could never tell, with Nora. She was quite capable of conversing with footprints. Or maybe it's dementia. It would be someday. They'd done those home DNA tests, and Nora had all the markers.

Nora smiled. "Deeper than yesterday, silly. I'm fat! Fat at last!" She lowered herself into her armchair with exaggerated effort.

Elsie ignored her, told her about the canvas she'd sold that morning, an imagined landscape of mist and sea and the hint of a seal in the waves. They talked for a while about art, and about the neighbours and their wilderness of raspberries.

"I really am heavier," Nora said when there was a pause.

Elsie tried to play along. "Because of the footprints?" In sand? "Maybe the sand was just softer."

"Perhaps." Nora had to acknowledge the possibility. "But I don't think so. I feel more massive."

"Massive?" It's not a word one would associate with Nora. Elsie cocked her head to the side to see around the curve of their little table. "You look the same."

"More massive. Heavier, sort of. Not bigger, necessarily."

Elsie rolled her eyes. "I know what massive means. Not all of us natives are ignorant." She did her best inscrutable Native American look. Quarter inscrutable, anyway. "You think all those books you leave lying around don't soak in?"

"Elsie! You've been reading my science fiction on the sly!"

"Just a little."

"I'm proud." Elsie could see that she really was touched. Was Nora's hand on hers heavier than usual? Maybe it was the power of suggestion; maybe she was pressing harder. It wasn't like her to fake, and her hand looked and felt as bony as ever.

"So what," Elsie asked. "The calcium in your bones is being replaced with ... iron?"

"Strontium! No. I don't know. Maybe the calcium is just laid down in a denser structure. Maybe all my fat is being replaced with muscle."

"So now we're back to fat again. You show me yours, and I'll show you mine."

Nora smiled, the same sweet smile that had made Elsie fall in love with her half a century ago, when Nora had been a young-ish professor, and Elsie an even younger Bohemian wanna-be, wandering through Portland State and trying to find herself. 'My found art', Elsie had called her, though she hadn't really started painting back then, not commercially.

Nora gathered up the plates and thudded into the kitchen. Was it really a thud, Elsie wondered, or just suggestion again? It didn't matter, because she was bringing out the cinnamon rolls, and it was rude to make her eat alone.

Crack! That had been the sound of the riser on their low front steps, cracking as Nora came back from the beach. She'd fallen, a fall that once would have risked fragile bone. By the time Elsie came rushing out, Nora was back on her feet, and she'd barely had a bruise. Elsie hadn't said a word, but she had gone into town soon after. She'd been upset again, frustrated at the mysterious weight gain that left her lover as thin as ever.

Nora sat gingerly on their little front porch sofa. It was wicker, and it trembled beneath her skinny buttocks before settling into place. She was heavier; even Elsie had to admit that, just as Nora had admitted that it wasn't fat. And it certainly wasn't strontium replacing the calcium in her bones. How would such a thing happen, and why? She could conceive of mechanisms, but they seemed unlikely. She hadn't troubled to look into it, and the latest *New Scientists* hadn't offered anything.

It was no harder to walk, to move, despite the groaning floorboards. She looked the same as ever. She felt good; better than ever, in fact. Why take it any further?

Elsie had, though, and when their new-ish Subaru pulled up, it sagged suspiciously at the back.

"Hey, Els," Nora called, taking care not to press too hard on the sofa's arm as she got up. "What's new in the big city?"

Elsie glowered at her, but motioned to the back of the car, now open. "Nothing. Any new gravitational anomalies? Help me get this stuff out."

"Same old, same old. You're the same, I'm old." Token laugh from Elsie. "I've just been sitting here communing with nature." Nora took a wide board from the back of the car, clearly destined to be the new riser. "What's the rest of this stuff?"

"Cinder blocks." Elsie took one out, put it by the stairs. "For under the house." She straightened, looked Nora in the eye. "If you keep ... communing, or whatever, you're going to crash through the floor." She bent to take another block from the car. "I'll have one of Heriberto's kids put them under the house. The older one – Luis. He's small enough to crawl under, but smart enough to put them somewhere useful." She dropped another block on the asphalt. It cracked at the corner, and the larger woman cursed.

"Come here." Nora motioned Elsie to sit on the steps, and stood behind to massage her shoulders, tight now with frustration.

"I don't know what this is, Nora," Elsie said eventually. "I don't know what to do." She sounded close to tears.

'There's nothing to do, Els." She stroked her fingers over Elsie's neck, over the little flecks of paint that seemed to find their way everywhere, as if Elsie painted in a wild flurry instead of calm brushtrokes. "Let's find Heriberto and ask him to send Luis over. We can tempt him with pie."

Elsie turned sideways, leaned her head against Nora's leg, a gesture that would once have sent the smaller woman stumbling back. "I know, Nora. I just worry. I'm just ..."

Afraid, Nora knew. Afraid of loss and of loneliness. "Where's that pie? These blocks aren't going to place themselves."

They had both done their research. Sometimes together, sometimes apart, but they'd both learned as much as they could about sudden weight gain, which was everything and nothing. Hundreds of diet plans and miracle pills. Nothing about bones made out of lead or barium or radium or anything else. Nora had refused go to a doctor about the weight. She said it wasn't a problem. Luis had put in three loads of blocks now, but the floor still creaked under Nora's feet. The old beach cottages weren't built for heavy use. How could that not be a problem?

Elsie worried about Nora using the toilet. She'd had Luis put two rows of blocks underneath, but what if it broke while she was sitting there? Maybe her bones were stronger; maybe they weren't. And what if Elsie couldn't pick her up? She wasn't sure she could lift Nora anymore.

They took the bed apart and put the mattress on the floor. It was hard for Elsie to get up in the morning, but Nora rolled right to her feet, where before she had been slow and careful. She weighed three times as much as Elsie. That was an estimate, since their scale didn't read that high, but the needle went all the way around, twice. That should have been 300 kilos. No healthy person weighed that much.

"Off to the beach?" Elsie had finally made it to her feet and put a robe on when Nora came back from the shower. Stray droplets ran off her bony frame, and the long grey hair she had tied up into a loose bun. The old grey heron. Elsie had painted her that way, wings barely open, standing cock-legged by an old log in Slab Creek, beak down, but the one visible eye looking off toward the sunset and the sea. "Say hi to the starfish for me."

"I will." Nora dressed, then kissed her on the shoulder, which was as high as she could reach. Her lips were cool and firm, but they warmed Elsie as they always had. "And the seals, and the mussels. Perhaps a whale or two, with luck."

"Leave out the mussels. I'm not that sociable." Elsie hugged her, held her tight, feeling the heavy solidity of her, where once she'd been almost afraid to touch, afraid a clumsy move would break her old bones. There were benefits to this mysterious new mass.

She followed Nora through the kitchen and the sitting room, to the front porch now built entirely of brick, the stairs replaced with stone. Beside the street, there was a line of paving stones, stretching from the house down to the beach. There was nobody around in winter, except Niles down at the corner, and he hadn't asked any questions. She'd seen him give a funny look at the footprints embedded in the asphalt of the street, but Elsie had just shrugged and said "Kids". She'd picked up the paving stones the same day.

Some of them were starting to crack.

It was difficult now for Nora to make her pilgrimages to the beach. Elsie's stepping stones had been a kind gesture, but they hadn't lasted. They were no more now than a jumble of splinters and gravel, pressed deep into the soil beside the street. It would be hard to explain when the neighbours came back in the spring. Even the boulders of the rip-rap showed wear, some of the wide steps cracked down the middle. Down on the sand, she sank quickly to her waist. It was like quicksand. Dry sand was relatively incompressible, but it flowed away under her feet until enough pressed around to support her weight laterally. It should have been hard to move, but it wasn't. It was less confining, even, than she imagined quicksand would have been. More like water. She moved languidly, gracefully, like a slow-motion dancer; synchronized swimming without the splash. It was a wonderful feeling, and she yearned to lie back and simply float in the sand like in the ocean. But she'd never floated in the real ocean; she was so skinny that she sank like a rock, and the real ocean was full of riptides and invisible currents. Beautiful but deadly, unless you were a seal. Better not to take the risk. She couldn't give up her seaside walks, though. Swims. Whatever they were.

She hadn't told Elsie about this new development. Her poor partner was frightened enough already. Better to just keep quiet and let nature (or whatever) take its course. They hadn't charted that course, hadn't bothered to record Nora's slow weight gain, to determine its rate. It was faster now, though, she was certain. Exponential, perhaps, which was interesting.

A plume of spray emerged suddenly from the deeper waters off the beach. "Hello, whale!" she called. It was hard to see much from waist depth, and she kicked her feet to surge up out of the sand and wave. "I weigh as much as you now," she said as she sank back. Her head went under, and she kicked again, suddenly desperate to see the surface, afraid she might not come up again. After a moment, she stabilized with her head well clear. She gasped for air, only to find her mouth already full of sand. It went gritty down her throat, and she coughed frantically, but most of it went down. Into her lungs, in part, she was sure. But it caused no trouble, no discomfort, and after a while, it came back up, in dribs and drabs with her rapid breath. No lasting harm, then, aside from a crust of sand on her lower lip, easily brushed off.

She swam down toward the water, but turned back when she saw a couple down the beach. Intrepid walkers out in the late winter cold, with storm winds in the offing; curious types, perhaps. Leery of discovery, she headed back for home, a casual backstroke taking her up the beach to the rocks and dry land.

"This can't go on," Elsie said as Nora paddled around in their tiny back yard.

"I know." Nora smiled and dipped under, and for a moment Elsie was angry again. Nora was literally sinking away from her, vanishing into the earth, and she thought it was fun. Her head popped back up, smiling like a clam.

"I can breathe." Nora grinned. "Or something. I'm so dense now that the sand in my lungs is like air." That made no sense to Elsie, but she'd stopped arguing. Nora said, "I don't even have to cough it out, anymore." She'd asked Elsie to cut all that beautiful gray hair to a short, sleek helmet - almost a crew cut - and the soil and sand pour off it now like water.

Nora caught hold of the concrete back step, gently, but still the surface powdered away under her fingertips. She hauled herself out, a sandy mermaid, and the step cracked under her weight. "Sorry."

"It's your house too," Elsie said, and they both sat quietly, thinking just how untrue that was.

"The moon is rising," Nora said at last.

"Is it?" Elsie asked dully.

"Look at me." Nora waved a hand. The last time she'd touched Elsie, it had left bruises. "I can feel it. The moon pulls me, makes me lighter."

There was hope yet, then, and Elsie look over at her. "How much lighter? Can you...?" She wasn't sure what she wanted. *Can you be normal?* But the moon rose every day. And then she got it. "You can only come up when the moon does." *You'll still be going.*

"That's right." Nora sounded sad and excited all at once. "But I'll still come and talk, like this."

"And then?" *When the pull of the moon isn't enough, what then? When the world pulls at you again and you can't rise, what then?*

"And then I'll be gone, Els. I don't..." She cleared her throat. "I don't think I'll be able to come back after that."

"Good," said Elsie. "I wouldn't want you to have to come back." It came out thick and angry, with the tears she never cried. Not in front of Nora. Elsie was the strong one, the practical one. The one who dealt with problems. When she cried, she cried in private, and she turned now to go inside, to keep her pain to herself. As she opened the door, she heard a sound, and she turned back to see Nora crying too, a broken expression on her face. The tears ran down her cheek, then dripped off. Where they hit the soil, they left little round drill holes. Where they hit the concrete, fine cracks spread out, until she was surrounded by an etching of fans.

Elsie sat down again, and they cried together, not touching.

As the moon set, Nora ebbed away like the tide, fighting up again every few hours, then flowing away. It was dark below, but surprisingly warm. The sand was soft, smooth, easy to swim through. She'd swum out under the houses to the beach, let herself sink there to the bedrock. She'd walked out to where it met ocean, but then retreated, afraid of what would happen if she stepped off the shelf to the depths below. She could see, even under the sand. Not light, perhaps, but something. Different frequencies, perhaps, above or below the visible range.

Unable to touch, they talked, after they'd accepted the inevitable, Nora with excitement and trepidation, Elsie with good old-fashioned fear and anger. And sadness, of course. Heartbreak, even. They'd been together half a century, had lived for each other, supplemented, complemented each other.

"We knew we didn't have long," she told Elsie. "Not at my age."

"You're not that old." It was a rote response.

"Maybe. But death was closing in."

"And now?"

"Now, I don't know. I don't know what this is any more than you do. But I feel good. Sharp. Strong."

"Not... not better, though?" Elsie's voice was a whisper, hopeful.

"No!" Nora was shocked. "I *love* you, Else. You know that." Elsie gave her a look of such gratitude that Nora longed to reach out and hug her. "If I could stay, I would."

They both nodded and pretended to accept it. Elsie pretended to be happy that Nora now faced adventure and life instead of decline and death.

Nora pretended to be sorry that a whole new world awaited her.

"No new theories?" asked Elsie, trying, as always, to face the problem head on.

"Nothing." It didn't matter. "Magic, maybe."

"You know as much about magic as I do about being a medicine man."

"Did the Tillamook Indians have medicine men?"

"How would I know? Grandpa never said. But everyone has medicine men – dancers, singers, priests who make up stories to explain the unexplainable."

"So? What do you say, medicine man?"

"Magic. Special gravity-moon magic only affect paleface woman."

Eventually, Nora became too dense for the sand to hold her up. It parted for her ever more easily, like water becoming fog, until she could no longer swim, but only jump and come crashing down to bedrock. They tried calling out to each other, but the sound didn't reach far through the sand. They tried intercoms, but the wires tangled and broke in roots and boulders and other subsoil obstacles. They hung a chain that Nora could use to climb back up from the depths, but when she pulled the back step off the house, they gave it up.

On Nora's last trip to the surface, Elsie gave her one of a pair of high-powered radios. Soon after, Nora found herself sinking into stone, the sand above as thin to her as air.

"I have to go now," Nora said into the radio, treading rock. She held the handset high in the sand to keep it safe, though that made it hard to hear.

“I know,” said Elsie after a long pause. “I miss you. I love you.”

“I love you too,” she called, giving one last kick to stay afloat in her sea of stone.

“Come back,” she heard as she sank at last, and her radio shattered on bedrock.

Elsie wanted to throw the radio against the fence and see it break, but she didn't. She was the practical one. Maybe Nora's radio still worked. Maybe some day when the moon and planets were in conjunction she would float up again and find it and give a call. Elsie would leave hers on for a couple of years, change the batteries on a schedule. Maybe Nora would just revert, and float back to the surface. Miraculously rejuvenated, of course. “When you wish, wish big,” Nora had always said.

Elsie didn't know what to do now. All these long months, she had avoided thinking of the end, even when it was clear, inevitable. She had never thought past the moment when they lost contact, when she had to admit that their worlds were separate. Forever, maybe.

She thought about Nora now, down in the rock somewhere, the weight of the world pressing on her shoulders. She was still in the crust, no doubt. But she'd said her density was an exponential function, so soon enough, she'd be through to the mantle. Presuming she could withstand the heat, she'd be floating around in convection currents. “Seeing the world,” she'd said, once. Then the core. And after that? Who could tell?

Elsie stepped through the steel-floored rooms now to the kitchen. She found she didn't much want to cook anymore. There was no one to cook for. Instead, she gathered canvas, easel, paint, and went out. In the street, she made her slow way down the trail of small footprints, beside the walkway of crumbled stone.

At the head of the street, she climbed the little rise and walked down it to set up her easel at the top of the rip-rap. At her back, a dark green bush waved little yellow flowers like brushes all dipped in sun. Waves curled and flattened, caressing the sand with soft, foamed fingers as they carried it out.

She painted as the sun sank. A beach, a sunset, footprints leading out. And there, just in the curl of one slow wave, the shadow of a heron.

About the story

This story started with literary theft. I was reading Jonathan Carroll's *After Silence*, which includes a brief story-within-a-story about a woman who gets skinnier and skinnier, and eventually floats away from her husband. Carroll doesn't do much more with it, but the idea intrigued me — the sudden and unexplained negation of physical laws for just one person.

I didn't tread too far from Carroll's original idea — my woman sinks instead of floating, which I thought allowed more opportunity for mystery and exploration. But while Carroll's story is a metaphor for marriage, mine is a stand-in for age-induced mental deterioration, with two women torn apart as one embarks on what seems to her a new adventure.

The story is set in a little coastal village where I spent many of my childhood summers, and now live full time. The house in question was once occupied by a lovely old woman who bears no other relation to the characters, and certainly didn't sink away into the sand.

I usually find titles easy, but this was an exception. I tried or considered almost a dozen before settling on this one.

Outburst

Earthlight sends jags of shadow crawling across the floor of the viewing bay, intangible reminders of the blowout that took #7 Arc, sent its occupants out into the dark. Killed my friends. Killed my parents. Killed my brother. They were at an Earthview, back when it was still a sick curiosity. No one comes here now, not in the year since the accident.

I miss Asil. He was pretty good, as brothers go. I've only had one, and now I wish I had him back. We were fighting, that night. We were always fighting. He was joining the EngineCrew, those idiot steampunk kids who go around pretending they can fix the station with rubber bands and tin foil. I was telling him what an idiot he was. I was always helpful like that. He didn't appreciate it. I guess that's how brothers are. It's hard, being a sister all on your own.

Afterward, the Engine Crew lashed up a workaround, closed off the #7 viewing bay and its ragged shards of plex, plastered off the bulkheads where the cracks were thin, filled the passageways with plastic tunnel where they're large, dug part of the route through the comet chunks still lashed to the outside of the station. You can still get round the circle that way, if you don't mind zigging and zagging through a maze filled with signs saying "Vacuum! Do not open!!" The #6 and #8 Arcs are lonely places these days.

I'm supposed to be checking for stress-fractures, or some shit like that, my weekly chore for the Committee for Space Station Renewal. No one really cares, though. They know it, and I know it, and if I want to spend my time looking out at the sharp plexteel petals of #7, no one's going to ask. Just like I don't ask why Marta spends a lot of time alone with a viewer and a feelie chip, or why Joaquin comes back bruised from #3 Arc, but goes back every week for more. We all know where the stress-fractures are. We just don't talk about it.

The Earth is a rich blue in the background, when I remember to look at it. I told the Moms I had memories of it – playing in the sand, swimming in the water. They liked that. I told Asil I had memories of their vids. They said that was me, running and splashing. I said I remembered. It doesn't matter now.

I don't even remember where that scene was supposed to be. Somewhere on the West side of Earth, I think, which is the simpler, plainer side with the wiggly bits. I don't know. The Moms used to complain about how it had all changed since the war, but it all looks the same to me – lots of blue, and some blobs of brown. I guess the night side is different, now that it's all dark.

They're taking bets now, whether we'll fall into night or day. I don't see that it matters. When the blowout happened, I don't guess Asil was thinking,

'Hey, at least I'm dying in Earthlight.' You never know, though. He was a romantic.

There's only so long you can stare out at disaster. Even teenagers have their limits, and I've met my quota for the day. I tap the 'No stress-fractures' icon on my wristpad under '#7 – viewing bay'. I've only looked through the ceiling plex, toward the station hub. I figure if the floor has fractures, I'll know about it soon enough. Besides, that side's toward the sun, and the plex is opaqued. Nothing to see there.

We keep all the hatches closed these days, when we remember. As I'm dogging shut the door to the viewing bay, my pad throbs. It's Jon, of course, sending a big smiley face and a note. 'Thanks for checking that out, Ef!' If there's any one thing about the EngineCrew that annoys me, it's the enthusiasm. What happened to plain old 'Tx', or just a check mark, or nothing at all? But hey, what's orbit decay when you have a smiley face?

It could be weeks, or months, even years, if the Crew can find enough rubber bands. Juana keep saying we could lift the orbit by using the Crew as reaction mass, but after the first hundred times, no joke is funny.

The hallways are empty at this time of day. I don't really know what 'time of day' means, but the Moms liked to say it. It's 02:34, which probably means some of the oldsters are sleeping. They sleep as much as they can, because what else can they do? My age group is probably down in the lounge, and I head that way. Probably I can find someone for a quick fuck. I don't much feel like it, but it's something to do. Maybe one of the guys, because I don't feel like doing any work.

My luck's in, I guess, because Vanya's around. He likes me, and he's up for it. He takes his time, and it's a good half hour before I have to confront my bleak existence again. Vanya talks like that – all poetry and existentialism. I figure we're all going to die anyway, and 'we're all going to die in a fiery crash to Earth' is not much different from 'we're all going to die in a massive blowout'.

"So, what do you think?" The afterglow of sex is starting to dim, but Vanya's question still catches me off-guard, and I go with an old standard.

"Oh man, you were the best. Dick big as a shuttle. Unstoppable. And that payload!" Vanya's thorough, but sometimes he needs a little hand-holding afterward. It's not my strong point; it always comes out sarcastic.

"Yeah, yeah, funny." I can see it working, though. He's squaring his shoulders unconsciously, as if a little sarcasm made him a better man. "No, I mean about joining the Crew."

"What, me?!" It's absurd, even offensive, and he should know better

"No, me." He did a little talking during sex, and it's coming clear that I didn't pay enough attention. "Were you listening at all?"

"Uh... sorry, big boy. Caught up in the moment." I was, too, in the sense that my brain was turned off so I wouldn't have to think. "Why, uh, why would you do that?"

He blinks slowly, sighs, rolls onto his back. "Forget it."

I'm tempted to. There's nothing I like less than talking about the Crew, but Vanya's a good guy, all in all. He's between me and Asil in age, was friends with both of us. So, alright. "You don't like the Crew anymore than I do."

He shrugs, and I can see it's on me to dig a little. I roll forward a little so that I'm up against his side. He's nice and warm, and a little sweaty. "So, what changed?" I ask. "Tell me."

That's all it takes. He shoves away a little, then rolls back so we're lying face to face, and he pushes one warm leg between my knees. I squeeze a little to encourage him.

"Here's the thing," he says. "I was talking with Jon, the other day. You know, scheduling chores, and all." I do all that by pad, but Vanya's a programmer, sort of, so maybe they need actual conversation. Plus, he's a lot more sociable than I am. Everyone is. "He said they've got a new idea."

"Oh, come on, Van." Now I'm on my back, and I'm looking for my panties out of the corner of my eye. The damn Crew *always* have a new idea. That's why they're so fucking optimistic. "Not one of those plans has ever worked out. Remember when urine venting was going to push us higher? Until they decided we need to retain the water? Or when they were going to slingshot us round the old Mir, as if we didn't outmass it by about a hundred to one? Or -"

"Yeah, okay, I got it."

"Or when -"

"I *got* it." He's irritated now, and the whole post-coital bliss thing has melted away into sticky rec-room pads and cold air. "Look, he's just saying that we have these little comet chunks stashed all over the rim. We can use *them*. Jon says that if we fire them just as they're perpendicular to the orbit, we'll be adding our rotational velocity to the mix. More velocity, more reaction."

There's something wrong with that, I'm pretty confident. "If we needed the water in urine, we sure as shit need the water in ice. Besides, how is it different than venting the piss to begin with?"

"I don't know. Nira did the calculations. Something about being a single mass, I think. And, yeah, we need the water, but only if we live."

I laugh. When was the last time any of us thought seriously about living? But Vanya's face gets tight, and I can see that he *is* thinking about it. That this severely stupid scheme is enough to give him hope, that he wants to believe it. That maybe believing it is his way of focusing, like for me it's sex, or staring out at #7 Arc.

Hope. The worst of Pandora's box of evils, except it wasn't her box at all, but a jar belonging to Prometheus' brother, and what the hell he was doing with a jar of evil stuff is anybody's guess. I'd damn the Greeks and their stupid stories, but I think someone already took care of that.

Vanya's no smarter than I am, and Jon's mostly just got the enthusiasm thing down. Nira's pretty sharp, though, even if she is a year younger than I am. So maybe the idea's not entirely stupid.

"You think dropping ice is going to save us? You think that's going to give us a future?" I get up and find my panties and cami in the corner. "You think anyone here has a future? *Any*one?" I'm shoving limbs into underwear as fast as I can, so I can leave. Because if it isn't stupid, and if there *is* a chance, then it's just crap, all of it. Because Asil wanted the chance, and he worked for it, and he's dead. And I'm still here, all alone.

I can hear Van calling as I grab my jumpsuit and booties and shove my way out of the room, but I can't hear him because I'm afraid of what he might say.

I've been spending time in #7 Arc. It's as far as I can get from Van, and as close to Asil and the Moms. I know they're not here. The Moms died of collapsed lungs and bubbles in their blood, and burned up in a tangle of arms and legs in Earth's atmosphere. Mom Edith's arm was caught up in Mom Angele's belt. I don't know if it was on purpose. The monitoring vids don't show that. Asil died the same way, but he got hurled up into higher orbit. The Moms bounced off the hub. Asil's still out there, somewhere. Maybe he's already come down. Maybe he reached escape velocity, and he's orbiting the sun all by himself. I like to think so. The Crew could probably tell me, but I've never asked. If he hadn't been hanging around with them... he'd still have died, I guess. I can't pin it on them. Just like I can't pin my survival on my stupid argument with him. I won't carry that guilt. I won't.

The #7 viewing bay itself is closed, of course. I went in it once, just to see. Wasted a whole lock worth of air, getting to it, and got a lecture for my trouble. Several lectures. There's nothing to see. Just a ceiling of clear plexteel with huge hole in it. They say a micrometeorite probably weakened the plex a day or so earlier. Nothing big. Just enough to cause a stress-fracture or two. Then, who knows. Faulty timing on a spin-jet, maybe. Or imbalance in the station rim. Maybe just loud music. Anything, really. That's what killed my family – anything.

Eventually, of course, they track me down. It's not tracking so much as finding. My pad's powered from the net, so anyone who wants to knows where I am. They're just giving me alone time. How much more alone can you get, when 99.99999999% of your species is dead, along with your whole home planet?

They send Nira, for some reason. I've never liked her much. She's smart, and she was Asil's best friend in the Crew. That's it, really. We're both pudgy and brown and tall. She's smart, I'm ... not as smart. She cares whether we live.

"Hey," she says. "People are worried about you, Efigenia." No pretense that it's her, at least.

"Oh well." Never give a centimeter, that's what Asil used to say. He said it sarcastically.

"The oldsters asked me to check on you."

"Huh."

"Van, too." She lets that sink in for a minute, like it's some kind of magic password to happiness, like I've been curled up in the corner waiting for Prince Charming to come kiss me. "Jon too. A bunch of folks, in fact. And the oldsters, of course." Because the oldsters aren't quite sure what to do with kids whose world has gone to shit, but they're sure it must be pretty traumatic.

"Well, gosh, thanks. Tell them I'm all sympathy-ed up now." I get up and wander over to a chair in the middle of the room, just to make clear that I use the whole space, not *just* the corners. "Dog the hatch when you go, why don't you?

Nira snorts, and it doesn't sound any cuter on her than when I do it. "Sympathy! What the hell for? Oh, wait, are your folks deader than my uncle, or his two kids, or Ms. Abramovic from down the corridor, or Mr. Luce, who taught me algebra?" She took me by surprise at first, but I see her dash a few tears off with one pudgy hand, and I can see she's just getting started. "Or maybe your life is harder than everybody else's? 'Cause, you know, all that sulking and shit you need to get done. So, yeah, sympathy. 'Cause you're the only one who lost Asil, aren't you?" The tears are streaming now, and the snot is starting to run. She wipes it on her sleeve, leaving a shiny trail down her cheek as she bends to put something gently on the deck. "Here's your sympathy, Ef. I hope you choke on it." And then she's gone.

I'm not entirely insensitive. It just takes me more time. Asil told me that once. I know, because it's right here on his wristpad, along with all the other stuff he ever texted me. It's tagged with 'LiS', which stands for 'Little Sister', though I can't see it right now because of the whole weeping thing.

I didn't know Nira had his pad. I didn't know why she would. I wanted to be angry that she didn't tell me, but then I read the stuff tagged with '♥'. Plus, I suppose that since the accident, I've been a touch on the bitchy side. So, fair enough, I guess.

I never knew they were so close. In the first years after the war, we still thought the station could survive, or the oldsters did. Things moved along about like usual. It was only after the accident, really, that it sank in. That's when things got loose. No classes, no rules. For me, no parents. We all put a lot of living into that time. It's hard to remember, sometimes, that things were ever different. For Asil and Nira, they were. He never had sex, I guess. Not with her. Maybe not ever. It's not in the wristpad, anyway. I don't know why it matters, but when I think about it, it hurts. It doesn't make sense, but that's life. That's what Asil would have said. That's life. 'Cause life is what it's all about.

I want to apologize, but when I make my way back to #1 Arc and Nira, the rec room is full of her EngineCrew friends. More than I've ever seen. It looks like all the youngsters in the station, and Van waves at me from one corner. Of course, Nira's right at the center, spouting off about orbits and mass and stuff, and why it won't work after all. And they're listening, nodding. Coming up with new ideas, like they haven't just been sentenced to death again. Asking what she thinks.

Like Asil did, I remind myself. She may be a genius, but she's not all brains. There's something else in there. She's still a kid, though, and she makes me walk all the way in, pretends not to see me until I'm standing at the edge of the circle like a supplicant, Asil's pad held in two hands to give back to her.

"Ef," she says at last, and I keep my anger in, because I'm being the bigger person here, and because I know that beneath all that bright exterior, she's hurting just as much as I am.

"Nira," I say, and that's as far as I get for a moment. She just watches while I get myself under control. I see Van getting up, and I know that if he puts an arm around me, I'll lose it for good. "I'm sorry," I manage at last, and offer the pad just before he reaches me.

Nira takes it, and I can see from her eyes that she's close to the brink too. I take her by the arm and pull her to her feet, and then I draw her in and hold her tight. I can feel her shaking, and I bury my face in her shoulder to hide the tears I just can't stop.

"I'm sorry, Nir," I whisper, and I don't know whether that's right, since that's what he called her. She just shakes more, so I guess it's alright. "I didn't know." About either of them. About Asil before he died, with my idiot questions about what he saw in the Crew. About Nira after he died, alone with her formulas and orbits and comet bits. "I didn't know."

She says something muffled, but it doesn't really matter, because I can't stop now. I whisper in her ear, as if the whole Crew isn't listening. "I'm so sorry. I just... I feel like I'm falling apart sometimes, without Asil and the Moms to hold me together. Like any moment now I'm going to start flying off in different directions. Like -" But now she's stiffening, and I've done it wrong again. "Oh, god, I'm sorry Nira. I'm so sorry."

I let her go and stumble back through a blur of tears. Someone's got me by the arm, and I just want to be alone, and I can smell Van's sweat as he wraps his arms around me and lets me cry.

"That's it!" Nira says, but she's excited, and I'm confused. "We break it up! We break the station up!" And then they're all yelling and clapping, and the noise cuts off, and Van and I are outside in the corridor.

"Well," he says, as he wipes my cheek and plants a kiss on my forehead. "Want to join the Crew with me?"

And somehow, despite the odds, despite the stupid human race, and the Crew's stupid optimism, I do.

About the story

Way back when, David Coverdale put out an album called White Snake, which included the song "Whitesnake". It couldn't have been any more Whitesnake, other than the fact that the band didn't yet exist. That song had a line I heard as "She'll help you make it in the crow light" which I thought sounded pretty interesting. I knew, deep down, that Mr. Coverdale was unlikely to have written a song with so few references to sex, but I like the way it sounded anyway.

Many years later, it occurred to me to figure out what he had actually said ("In the shadows of the dark night / She help you make it in the cold light") and, having succumbed to disappointment, decided to do something with what should have been.

I sat down to write a story about crow light. My first attempt ended up as "A Conversion of Crows", about magic and ruins on a place like the Oregon coast. While I liked it, it veered pretty far from what I'd intended originally, so I sat down to write another. This one brought in more of the dark night, which led to a decaying space station, and "Outburst". I liked it, but it still wasn't what I'd intended, so some day I'll sit down and give it another try. Eventually, there will be a story legitimately called "In the Crow Light". I'm eager to see what it's about.

The Irrigation Ditch

She'd shifted a cottage-weight of stone, lifted uncounted shovelfuls of soil, dug her way with mattock and sweat and bruised fingers. Before her, beneath her, all she had was a hole. The same as when she'd lifted that first shovel load, the same as she'd have after countless more.

She leaned over, let the sweat run slowly from her forehead to the tip of her nose, to gather there, in a swelling, glittering bulge just out of focus, until it fell at last into the hole and was lost in the dirt, became part of it. *Salting the fields*, she thought, though it was a hole, not a field, and not much of a hole. Forearm deep, about as broad, it wavered ambiguously across the hillside, dropping here to avoid a boulder, there to curve around a tree, turning on itself from time to time like a snake slowly undulating down the slope.

"Ditch," she said, when she had her breath back. "You're a ditch." A hole was just an empty space, a place where something wasn't. Bigger or smaller, it stayed the same, of no fixed dimension, but essentially negative. A ditch, now, had purpose, definition. A beginning and end.

She looked down the hill, to where the land flattened out, and trees clustered close to a cozy stone-weight of cottage, a round-cornered pile of shale and mud, with square-ish gaps for windows and a cheery little chimney at the far end. Inside, she knew, Rewk would be making jam or pickling carrots, or whatever it was the season for. Whatever it would be the season to eat, when winter fell heavy, and the windows wore wooden shutters laced snug with ice, and they sat by the fire under a warm blanket. The ditch began there, in Rewk's kitchen garden, with its ordered plots and raised beds and mysterious frilly greens, some sharp, some bitter, some crisp, like Rewk himself.

The ditch began down there, in Rewk's aching back and swollen joints and stolid silence. The channel would end there, once she had it dug, would peter out into little rills that stretched thin, wriggling fingers across the garden and laughed in the face of the well and its ever-deeper water, its ever-longer rope. But only if she got it dug.

She looked up the slope, stretching her back to straighten cramped muscles. She was about halfway, she thought. Halfway to the top, to the little cwm and its lake, to cool, clear water that filled the little hillside depression and trickled slowly out in just the wrong place.

Halfway, not partway. Halfway was a marker, a symbol, a turning point. At halfway, most of the work was done, the decision was made, the effort committed. At halfway, you had something. Not just a hole, but a ditch. You had a thing that came into being, once you called it by its name.

"Names are important," Rewk would say. "This is mustard, this is collard, this is kale. They're not just leafy green things." Though they were all leafy and green, and they all looked similar until he put them in his pans and turned them by magic into food.

She would smile and nod and let his magic melt down her throat while she talked about digging and channels and how important it was to irrigate the orchard that she hadn't planted, and how lake water was purer than well water, and how of course it wasn't just for his little garden, and wouldn't *that* be waste of time and effort.

Ends were the opposite of holes. A hole was a hole as soon as you started. An end was an end only when you stopped. Names were tricky that way; they had rules, and if you didn't play by the rules, you got something else entirely, no matter what you called it. The rules right now, she admitted, called for more digging.

He worked by the window, where the light was fair, though it would have been better by the southern doorway to his right, or outside, on the west side of the cottage where the sun angled down through pine trees with a warm, shady light. At the window, he could keep watch on the bubbling stew, and his eyesight was still strong enough to see the quick, sharp stitches he made in one of Derla's shirts.

He could see her past the hemlocks, as she dug her way slowly, tirelessly, up through the hill toward water. Like a mole, coming up from the earth into a sudden and unexpected rainstorm that would leave it drenched, refreshed, victorious.

He wondered, as he watched her, if he should make another token gesture to help, or another, firmer effort to convince her that fruit trees didn't need special irrigation, and that they would in any case be easier to grow on the flat. Then she would say something about grapes, and he would ask what they would do with grapes when neither of them liked wine, and she would mutter about taking wine to market in Hatherton, and it would go on until one of them stomped angry out of the house, or they gave it up and curled warm together like some complex braided bread that never went stale.

He pricked his finger as he watched her, and transferred the injured digit to his mouth until it should stop bleeding and putting Derla's shirt at risk of spots. He sucked on the fingertip, spreading warm saliva around and over it. It felt good on the perennially swollen knuckle. If only his mouth were bigger, he sometimes thought he would spend his whole day with his hands in his mouth like a baby. A pot of warm water might do the same, but how could he work with wet hands? And she would notice. She always noticed.

Already he suspected her of some buried motive for her ditch – a waterwheel, perhaps, or a duckpond. Something helpful and impractical that would tire her and knot her muscles and leave her limp and loving and righteous, until some day, in an argument about grapes, it would come out and he would feel cruel and hard and sorry all at once, and one of them would go off to Hatherton. One day, he suspected, one of them would not come back. Or they would come back, and no one would be home. And what was home without Derla? Just a word, just a place, not a thing, not a warm spot that your heart nestled into without even knowing it was there.

He took his finger out of its damp, warm resting place, and examined it critically. Slick with an old man's slobber, but not bloody. He gave it a tentative squeeze, and it smarted, but no blood flowed. Good enough. Pain was nothing but an ugly name for the scouts your body sent out to look for trouble. As you got older, they reported more and more frequently, until there was a constant stream of them in and out of the command tent. One more would make no difference.

"I'm over halfway," she announced that evening, over a thick stew of barley and lentils and chewy parsnip. Over halfway. It was definite when you said it out loud, irrevocable. You'd staked your claim, made your boast, like an empress asserting rights over land she'd seen through a window. You had to make good, or be forsworn, be shunned as a braggart, deposed in favor of some more modest ruler.

"That's good," he said, and she could see the cogs turning, the careful calculations. "Maybe I can come and help tomorrow."

She turned to her stew, sought quietude in its savour. It must be hard, she thought, to be strong and capable, and yet be overcome by such an insidious enemy as time. There was a pride in strength that she had never seen him display, never known until nature had taken the strength slowly away, leaving nothing but gnarled joints and empty confidence. She rolled her own shoulders, so broad now, so tight with work that he could no longer do, though he was younger by a year or two.

"Yes," she blurted, as the silence lengthened and she looked up to see brown eyes fixed on her. "Yes, come up with lunch." She could see the wince he tried to control, could see the tension in fingers that would never curl around a shovel again. That had never, it seemed to her, been entirely straight, entirely pain-free. "There's a gully there, where the lake overflows when the rain is hard. I was thinking of incorporating it, but I'm not sure how. You could help me decide, with your eye for detail. Maybe draw it for me," to indicate that of course twisted hands were no obstacle, that he could do everything she needed.

"Of course," he said, and reached out to squeeze her hard, rough hand with his smooth, knobbly one. It felt like a sprig of huckleberry – twigs covered with round berries full of juice and color, if only they could get free of their confinement. She lifted it to her lips and took a berry in her mouth to see the light spring up in his eyes. To her surprise, she felt a heat of her own, and they left the stew to itself as they sank onto warm blankets and a slow, easy exploration of this new sun – always bright, always hot, even for a woman who'd felt it many, many times before.

The bread was done, though it had used the last of their ready flour. With a waterwheel, they could do better than the coarse powder he coaxed from his small hand mill. It worked well enough to repay the winter he'd spent filing grooves in the lower stone, the quern, but even the simple rotary motion of the upper stone left his hands cramped and tight. It might have been better, he smiled, had they not been broken, or had they healed better. 'Crooked hands for a crooked man,' they'd said when they broke them, and who was to say they weren't right? One man's crooked was another man's curved, and one man's curved was another man's straight.

He took the loaves from the oven, breathed in their rich, yeasty fragrance. He set two on the counter to cool, wrapped the other in a coarse cloth, and laid it at the top of his little woven pannier. Cold bean salad, hot bread, and there would be fresh water from the lake. He tucked spoons under the light blanket. Derla would deride it as a foolish, townish extravagance, but she liked extravagance, for all her homespun simplicity.

The day was hot, and the pannier rode uncomfortably on his back, but he followed the route of the ditch up the hill, crossing back and forth, back and forth, waving to Derla at the near points, though she pretended not to see him, redoubling her efforts as if some hidden overseer were watching for sloth.

He cut across the last switchback, climbing straight up the hill toward the swing of her heavy mattock. It looked like a little less than halfway, but she had said half, and so it therefore was. He paused to wipe the sweat from his brow, and to admire the muscle across her broad back and still-slender hips.

"Ho there, young laborer. Have you time for a simple provider of provender, or must you toil until nightfall?"

"You got food, I got hunger," she said, setting her mattock on long grass and turning to face him. "And I'll eat *again* at night. That's how we are, out here in the foothills."

"And a fine breed you are," he agreed. "How about that tree over there?" A generous chestnut, it spread its branches wide and green over a flattish area at its base. He took assent for granted, and wandered over to set his pannier down and spread the little blanket wide.

"Oh my goodness," she exclaimed with a cultured voice he rarely heard and had never quite traced. "What a fine establishment you run."

"At your service, my lady." He laid down the spoons, the bowl of salad, and, with a flourish that wafted its scent her way, the fresh-baked bread. "We lack only water." He held up a generous gourd. "If you could..."

"Come with me," she said, herself again. "We can cool off in the lake, and I can show you that gully."

He bowed and tucked the gourd under one arm as she led off up the hill. She was a better engineer than he'd ever been, though less of an artist. Her sketches were all angles and calculations that left his head swimming. His were less accurate, but, she said, more true to life. Since they both knew the question of the gully to be one more of emotion than calculation, he supposed his skills might suffice.

They'd stopped near the crest of the hill to discuss the gully, to breathe, to admire the view. The cottage was a patch of grey stone amongst the green of wood and meadow, and she thought as always that it would have made a fine site for a manor, if only a wealthy merchant had cared to live out here near the mountains and far from culture.

And if they had, she would be elsewhere, in another cottage that functioned as her manor, to protect everything she held dear, and keep herself and it from harm.

They climbed the last few steps hand in hand, waiting for the moment when a vista of grass and rock and sky turned suddenly, surprisingly, silver, and then blue, and then clear, and the lake water seemed to vanish entirely, leaving a bed of rocks and algae and ducks floating on little ripples of air until the wind blew, or a duck flew off, and the water was back in a shimmer of grey and green.

They looked out over the mirror-smooth surface of the lake, and the wind blew, and the ducks flew off, and a man rose out of the water.

Rewk spread his arms and stepped in front of her, fists knotted, as if either of them had ever fought, had ever held a weapon more dangerous than the gourd still gripped ludicrously in Rewk's left hand. As if a naked man were a threat, no matter how the water dripped from short hair onto wide shoulders and down over muscle to fall into the lake that even now he made his slow, sure way out of.

He smiled, a confident, knowing smile that sent shivers down her spine, and a chill through her heart. It was the smile of a man who knew what he wanted, and got it. The kind of smile she'd changed her life to avoid.

"What are you doing here?" asked Rewk, always blunt, always focused.

"Is it your lake?" the man asked as he wiped water from hair and chest and arms and reached for a fine grey blouse she saw now, draped over a nearby stone.

"No," Rewk admitted. "You just... surprised us."

"Surprise can be good. Revelatory." Muddy brown eyes caught hers and held them until he bent to pull on smallclothes and trousers.

"Sometimes good, sometimes bad. It doesn't matter what you call it." Rewk argued a point, that, she thought, no one had raised.

"Welcome," she said, stepping forward. "Though, as you point out, the lake isn't ours. Not formally."

"Formalities aren't everything," the man said as he sat on a dry rock to slip on socks and shoes. "If you call it yours, it's yours."

"No one said that," said Rewk sharply, still arguing his own track.

"So long as no one says different," the other added, with a wink at Derla that brought back forgotten nights of torches and stars, lively dinners, intimate dances. "I'm Merro."

She saw Rewk's look of suspicion and something more, and took Merro's outstretched hand in her own. It was hard, strong, dry, and it squeezed her heart with a gentle pressure. "Derla," she managed. *Now, anyway,* and she knew it was a quirking smile and dark eyes that made her think it.

He tipped his head toward Rewk, with a twitch of eyebrow toward Derla to share the joke.

"Rewk," said Rewk. He didn't offer his hand.

"A man of few words, but valuable ones."

Rewk said nothing.

"We were just coming for water," she said, taking the gourd still dangling from Rewk's hand.

"Let me," Merro said, taking the gourd and dipping it elegantly into the lake without getting so much as a finger wet, though his clothes were already damp from wet skin. "Shall we?" And then they were following him back down the hill to a picnic blanket and salad and still-warm bread and fresh fruit from a pack that somehow materialized on Merro's back.

In the morning, Rewk was up before dawn. "Just in case," he told her. She'd invited the stranger to sleep under the eaves, but he'd looked up at the clear blue sky and said the meadow was fine with him. And there he was, a still, dark shape against the lightening sky, with his back against a tree and his legs up on his pack.

"Morning," Rewk said.

"Morning," Merro replied, and said no more.

Rewk grimaced. In the old days, he'd have known how to winkle the stranger's secrets out from under his tongue with just a smile. In the older, darker days, when he'd known how to speak. When had he become so taciturn, so quiet that even a greeting was an effort?

The stranger seemed content to watch the sun lighten the sky beyond the hill, to let the rose-tinged clouds give false light to dark hair. Muscles moved beneath rich skin as he shifted to make space beside the tree without a word.

Rewk sat, slowly, a pace away. "You're far from home," he said at last.

"Am I?"

"Anyone who's here is far from home," Rewk said, knowing that he gave away more of himself than he learned.

"Home is what you make it," the stranger said. "Or what you make of it, perhaps."

"You're a fine one for words." And dangerous for it.

"You've spied that out, have you?"

And there it was – the knife behind the back, and the chill down his spine. Rewk's twisted fingers hurt as he failed to keep them from clutching at the grass.

"What do you want?" He'd already paid the price, paid with pain in past and present and future, paid with memory and absence.

"Little enough," the stranger said, and white teeth gleamed against brown skin. "Just to know you and pass through your lands."

"You know me well enough," and more. "How about you skip straight to passing through?"

Merro chuckled. "We've barely met; I'm sure there's more we can learn about each other." He smiled a smile so full of hunger that Rewk twitched back, remembering the hot feel of hands and breath and muscle against his back.

He swallowed and rose. "You know me enough to know I don't want that."

"Perhaps. Perhaps Derla does." The smile was menacing now.

"Try to find out." If there was one thing Derla had in plenty, it was constancy. "Try, and then leave."

Merro winked, and settled back against his tree. "Fair enough. We'll see whether Derla knows herself as well as you do." And though there was a message there as well, Rewk turned his back on it and looked to gardens and stews and things that could be predicted, that were safe, that had no secrets to divulge.

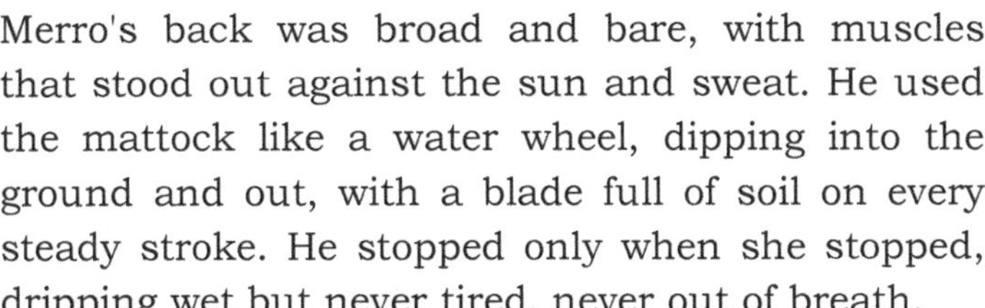

Merro's back was broad and bare, with muscles that stood out against the sun and sweat. He used the mattock like a water wheel, dipping into the ground and out, with a blade full of soil on every steady stroke. He stopped only when she stopped, dripping wet but never tired, never out of breath.

"You're like a machine," she said at last, when she couldn't lift another shovelful, when arms like soft wax refused to rise again. Already in one morning, they'd done more work than she had in two days.

"It's the steam," he said, and turned to wave toward where a mist rose off her wet blouse and faded into nothing. "It drives the pistons that do the work."

"Well, your linkages are certainly well made," she said, and only then wondered whether she had already given herself away.

He winked as if she'd said nothing more than flattery, and made a joke of flexing muscles. "They'd have to be, to keep up with your pace." He dropped the mattock and wiped a hand across his brow and the short, tight ringlets that held beads of sweat to his scalp like pearls. "If this was a test, I concede." As if a fit, youngish man could be bested by an old woman whose only virtue was practice.

"No test. Already you've put me days ahead of schedule, and we've nothing to offer in exchange."

"A chance to rest from wandering, to eat real food, talk with real people. That's not nothing."

"Little enough, if you call this a rest." She nodded toward the slope, and the lake that lay behind it. "Real water, in any case."

He followed her up the hill. “That lake water,” he agreed, “finer than the finest Bourgnon vintage...”

“...and just as sweet,” she laughed, completing the joke. A joke she'd not heard in years, a joke that relied on an urban view of water as a flat, lifeless commodity rather than a sweet, heavy gift from the mountains.

He climbed past her, walking straight into the cold clear chill of the lake, letting it soak into his thin trousers and plaster them to his skin.

“Your boots will be wet,” she said unnecessarily.

He sank slowly into the water up to his neck before turning back toward her to climb out. “I'll stay until they're dry, then. They needed a good cleaning anyway.” He stood dripping in front of her, and she noticed for the first time that his brown eyes were level with hers. “Sometimes it's good to wash away the remnants of the past.” He set on a rock to pull the boots off, as if his words hadn't struck her to the core and taken away her power of speech. He swished the boots this way and that, canvas and rope and cork floating slowly back and forth while her thoughts raced. “Even a past that's bright and plush.”

“Who are you?” she asked, her tongue freed from its chains by a gaze that weighed her up and knew her worth exactly.

“Just a visitor. Just passing through.” His dark eyes belied the easy tone, held her pinned to the rocky shoreline that hid a ditch and a slope and a home.

“And will you go back, when you're done passing?” Back to a city, and soft cloth, and groaning tables of every kind of food, and whispers in dark hallways.

"That depends," he said, and set the boots to dry on a warm stone. Water seeped out to leave a dark stain across the stone. "Let's see about that digging, why don't we?"

The ditch was done. The channel, as Derla called it, with the gully incorporated, and water flowing clear and quick from the lake and into his garden. It fed his plants and slipped past them, to collect in a little pond at the edge of the forest. Already, it drew deer and foxes and little glitterbirds that hovered just above the surface, their wings causing ripples that never quite seemed to fade, but never reached the shore.

They'd looked at his drawings, she and Merro, and talked knowledgeably about the rate of flow, and the thrust of water, and how the walls would get slippery and might start to fall. And every now and then they'd turn to him and smile or wink, and say how they couldn't have done it without him. And what exactly had they done?

They were outside now, in the rain. Merro had come in and seen him grinding his slow, painful way through a handful of wheat. He'd taken over without a word, just taking Rewk's old, twisted hands in his warm, strong, straight ones and setting them aside with a look that could have meant anything. He'd had a full bag ground within the hour, and it took that long for Rewk's heart to stop its nervous flutter.

Merro had said nothing at lunch, and yet somehow Derla had seen the bag of flour in their little larder. She'd looked at the stranger's hands, on which no speck of white remained, and looked at Rewk like her heart was breaking.

He'd been sharp with them both throughout the meal, until his acid tongue had driven them out to work in a foggy drizzle, shoulder to shoulder in the gully installing board and batten to guard against slippage. And he was here, warm and dry and alone, with only a bowl of beans to drain and soak and drain again.

It had been easier, in the old days. Then, he'd had clear goals, and a purpose, and a role. The role had been important. He'd clung to it, in the dark times, let *it* define him, rather than the things he did and that were done to him. It had all been the role, not him at all. He'd saved lives. He knew he had. They'd given him a medal, or rather shown it to him and then taken it away – for safety, for secrecy. They'd given him money instead. A lot of money. Gold and silver and pitying looks and kind words. They'd avoided him, in the barracks, in the streets, in the offices of the ministry, let their guilt eat at them until it hurt to see them watch him, to force their eyes to look even as it hurt their souls to do it.

And why not? They'd been the ones to send him. He'd volunteered, yes, along with some of the other boys, when it had been clear they needed boys. Slight ones, smart ones. And they'd picked him, the slightest, the smartest.

"I'm to be a spy," he'd said at last, putting a name to it. And they'd grasped at the straw.

"Yes," they said, "a spy. To gather their secrets and communicate them to us. We'll put you with the enemy's high command. We have a way."

It had been exciting, heroic.

"You understand what you'd be doing?" they asked, though he could see the words turn bitter in their mouths.

"Of course." There was nothing new about that, though he'd never done it before, never wanted to.

"We ... it's ... there's no other way," the general had gasped, as though the weight of guilt were crushing her flat.

"It's nothing to me," he'd said. Brave, heroic. Smiling in the face of danger. And this wasn't even that.

"It's revolting," said the minister, standing. "I'll have nothing more to do with it." The door clicked quietly behind him.

"It's not revolting," he'd said, confused. "The sergeant and Peter the cooper do it all the time. So do Lieutenant Ekar and Captain Laro. So do..."

The general had laughed until she looked like she might cry. "No need to list *all* the fraternization that's not supposed to happen between ranks."

"I watched. I know how to do it. I asked Laro if I could try, but he said no." It hadn't looked hard.

"It's not that. It's your age." She'd taken his hand and squeezed it tight. "If there were any other way..."

"But catamites have to be young, don't they?" And then she really had cried, and he'd been taken off by a hard-eyed sergeant.

"You forget all that," the man had said. "You're doing your duty, son. Don't ever question that. We have a job needs doing, and you're the man for it, young as you are. Like it or not, you do that job, and don't ever forget why. You're doing it for your mother, your father, your uncle. For that general in there. You're even doing it for me. When the war's over, you come find me, and I'll buy you a beer, and you'll tell me it wasn't so bad, eh?"

He'd remembered that beer all through the war, through the good times, and the bad, through the parts he liked, and the parts he didn't. And mostly it wasn't bad.

He'd never found the sergeant, of course. Their forces had been decimated, and decimated again, and again, until by the time they'd won, almost half the population was in the army, and over half the army had died. But they'd won, and he'd played his role, and the only hard part had been the end.

"You set him on edge," she said as they climbed up to the lake to wash off the mud. "He's not usually quite so brusque." Harsh, sometimes, and direct. But kind. Always kind.

"Well," Merro said, helping her peel off a sodden, mud-slimed blouse. "I can see why he'd be jealous." Did his hands slide a little too closely along her arms? Did they want to?

"Jealous! Don't be ridiculous." And yet here she was, waist deep in a lake in just her undershirt and small clothes with another man. They were both muddy and tired, of course, but she hadn't thought twice about it. Hadn't thought for a moment about how it might look to Rewk. But she'd thought about how Merro might look to her. Almost against her will, her eyes slid back to him, to his strong shoulders and tight-curled hair. He smiled.

"I'm going to swim," she blurted, and threw herself almost sideways into the cold water. She stroked hard, straight and sure with the form she'd learned in the mill-pond back home, when she'd been young enough that being friends with the miller's daughter felt natural.

"You're a natural," came Merro's voice when she stopped halfway across to tread water. He swam so smoothly she hadn't even heard him. "You know, they do this competitively in some places."

"Do what?" Not drown?

"Swim. They race. Only the upper classes, of course. And canal pilots. No one else has the time to learn non-essential skills." And she wasn't a canal pilot.

"Do they." She imbued the words with as much disinterest as she could manage, though the clear water showed that he'd taken the time to drop his own clothes, all of them. He kicked his feet, swept his arms, and she felt the water wash across her.

"What's at the bottom?" he asked, and before she could answer, he'd turned to jackknife cleanly into the water, buttocks and long legs rising up above the water before slowly, sleekly sliding in.

"You," she whispered. Hadn't he come out of the lake to begin with? But he hadn't vanished. She could see him down there, his wavering, flickering form straightening out to scull along the bottom and through the boulders that lay there.

She turned away and continued her swim, stopping to rest at the other side, and watching his dark head pop up through the rain that had turned to mist. He swam back toward their clothes, and once she'd rested, so did she.

"Gold," he said as she stroked close. "Jewels. Magic swords. Caves and creatures."

"Rocks, in other words." She came up out of the water, and turned away to wring as much of the water as she could out of her undershirt. It clung to her anyway, cold and wet.

"Not as hard as you," he said. "Or me, come to that. We're tough, both of us. Not like Rewk."

"He's harder than the two of us put together," she said startled. She blushed, as if she'd forgotten all about him, as if she'd been caught at something. "He's granite. You're just marble. Pretty, but soft." And what was she? Sandstone, so easily worn away? She pulled her blouse over her head, fighting with the wet cloth. This time, he didn't help.

"You'd be surprised," he said. "Rewk may be more fragile than you think."

"What would you know about him?" And how had they gotten here? How had hard work together turned into an analysis of personalities?

He smiled. "What do *you* know?" He walked out of the water, gathering up his neatly folded clothes from the side of the lake and disappearing over the edge of the slope, leaving her with just an echo, and a doubt.

What did she know about him? That he'd been a soldier. That he'd built this cabin when he was younger and stronger, that he'd shopped in Hatherton when she'd been passing through, looking for a place to hide from obligation and society. That he'd done something that ate at him, something that had brought him enough money to live on, something that made him cry sometimes at night when he pretended to go out to pee.

"That he's a good man," she told the lake, and herself. "That he's never asked for anything. That he's never done me wrong." Even when they argued, when they were angry, he'd always played fair. Never undercut her, never tried to bind her to him with word or deed. That was why she had stayed, all those times they'd fought over stupid little things, imagined slights. Why she'd always come back, always fearing that he might have gone on. "That he loves me."

And that she was here, half-naked, half-disappointed that Merro had taken his muscle and his youth and his beauty and left her to feel wretched and cold, and to know that she was wrong.

He came in the door naked, his clothes a dripping pile before him. "Mind if I hang these to dry?" he asked, turning to the hearth.

Rewk closed his eyes, but he still saw taut muscles, a chest dripping water down a hard belly. "You and Derla are done, are you?" He tried to keep his voice flat, disinterested, but it came out harsh and bitter. "With your work."

Merro stayed silent, making a lean-to out of twigs and his shirt. Done, he rose and turned, still naked, still perfect. "Derla and I haven't even started, Kell. You know that."

Rewk froze, feeling the blood drain out of his face and shoulders to hear the name he'd tried so hard to kill, to bury. He didn't react when the other man stepped close, took him by the hand.

"Your fingers are cold," Merro said. "Let me help." He slid Rewk's hand along his chest, held it tight under his arm, surprisingly warm despite the rain that still clung in drops.

"How...?" There were too many questions to ask. "Who...?"

"Does it matter? One name's as good as another." Without letting loose Rewk's hand, he pulled a stool close, settled on it. He took Rewk's other hand, slipped it between warm thighs. "What matters is what we do, don't you think?"

And he knew. Clearly he knew, as he took Rewk's gnarled hand from beneath his arm and kneaded it, finding the knots and lumps of poorly healed bone and pressing heat into them until they felt almost straight. He knew exactly what Rewk was, and what he had done.

The relief surprised him. He'd thought the memories locked up tight – safe and secret in locked chests in locked rooms in deep vaults in his mind. Yet here they were, exposed and open, and he felt no fear, only respite.

"It's alright," said Merro, and kissed him. It was warm and soft and comforting, and he sank into it. There had been other days, other kisses, other arms around him. Others who had cared for him.

Abruptly, he pushed Merro away. "No." Though his heart trembled, his voice was firm and hard.

"Are you sure?" Merro asked, twining his young fingers into Rewk's damaged ones.

"I'm sure." He pulled his hands free.

"You can't hurt me, Kell."

"Don't be so sure. I'm a professional."

"I'm sure," Merro echoed. "I know you."

"Do you?" And if so, whom did he know? The bold, foolish boy who'd learned the enemy's plans from inside their commander's bed? The dutiful adolescent who'd passed the plans along to other, older spies with the same hands that evoked pleasure? The young man who'd sat silent as soldiers held him down and his lover broke his fingers one by one while an army made its last stand around him? The broken soul who'd watched with his hands in bandages and tears in his eyes as they strung a man up and taunted the death erection on his dangling, naked corpse?

"I know all I need to," Merro said softly.

"So do I," said Rewk, and turned away.

Derla stood at the door, little rills running down her face. He took her in his arms, felt her flinch, then shudder, then relax. "Rewk," she said into his shoulder. "I'm so sorry."

"We're a sorry lot," was all he said. Over his shoulder, he said to Merro, "You'll be gone in the morning." There was no answer as they moved awkwardly into the little bedroom, arms still tight around each other.

He told her the whole story that night.

"I've heard of you," she said. "You're the one who won the war for us."

"Yes," he said. "I'm sorry."

She held him tight. "I didn't realize you were so young," she said after a while. "I mean, not you..."

"The spy."

"Yes."

"No. That was the secret. Even after the war. They felt guilty."

"They should have. Of course they did. Sending a child. A *child!*"

He nodded, his head warm against her breasts. "It was wrong. I know that now. But what choice did they have? That's what he liked."

"It was wrong. That's what we fought against!"

"Pedophiles?"

"No! Yes! That's what they said about him, to whip us up. What *we* said."

He shrugged. "He was kind to me."

"Except..."

"I knew what I was getting into. I wasn't that young."

"Too young!"

"Yes. It happens, though."

"Not like this. Not..."

"Procured?"

"It was wrong. And they sent you off..." She began to cry.

"With nothing but a sackful of money," he said, raising his head to kiss her.

"We can change that," she said. "I know people."

"Don't think about it."

"No, really. My father is ... was a minister."

He stilled. "A minister." He remembered a stern face, the click of a door as a man washed his conscience clean.

"During the war. After, he quit politics. He started a school. And an orphanage." He felt her breathing stop. "Oh!" she gasped. "Oh. Oh." He held her as the gasps turned to sobs.

"It doesn't matter," he said.

"It does," she mumbled. "It does. He made you a ..."

"A catamite," he said calmly. "A spy. And a traitor." He smiled. "I did too. It doesn't matter. Whatever name you put to it, I did what I did. I am what I am."

"It does matter," she insisted, rising above him. "You're not just some leafy green thing. You're Rewk. And I love you." And though she didn't put a name to it, she suited action to words, until she collapsed shuddering on top of him and held him as tight as she could.

In the morning, Merro was gone, as though he'd never been. The cottage felt larger without him, less oppressive without his presence, though the day was hot, and the air was still and close.

"Was he someone you knew?" she asked as he opened a sluice to let water into the garden.

"No. Maybe someone from intelligence, checking that I hadn't spilled the secret." Though he had spilled it to her thoroughly now, and doubtless would continue to spill for years to come.

"Or maybe a lake spirit, come to bring our secrets out in the open," she said. Or her father, topping off payments on an endless debt.

He smiled. "We'll have a good crop this year," he said. "I may have to expand the garden." He turned to admire the lake water as it ran down the hill and into his greens. Whatever she'd built it for, it would work wonders on their salads.

"It's an irrigation ditch," she said, calling it what it was, what she had always meant it to be.

"Is it?" He nodded approvingly. "It's a good one. I was thinking, though. How would you feel about a little waterwheel? My hands aren't what they used to be."

"That's okay," she said, taking his swollen hand in hers. "Right now it's a ditch. But we can always rename it."

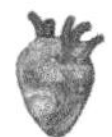

About the story

I was playing around with the idea of conjuring with names, and the search for the right name. I wanted to write a Richard Grant-type story with Patricia McKillip-style prose, though of course what emerged was something different. It pretty quickly it emerged that the two main characters had secret histories. While I started with the image of a person emerging from the lake, that eventually faded to a supporting role.

Dragons I Have Slain

I collect dragon tears. It isn't difficult; they're insidious and subtle, and they seep through my armor and into my skin like ink, leaving me stained, soiled, sorrowful — a human map of misery. The Dragon Atlas, I call it — marked with the precise locations of honor and shame.

Dragons cry for the same reasons we do — pain, heartache, joy. We think of them as wise and cold, but wisdom is no antidote to empathy. Dragons are kings of empathy. That's what makes killing them so hard.

There was Vyurfang, short for something unpronounceable in dragon-tongue. I stood on his chest, his broken limbs splayed out across the rocks, the point of my longsword slipped between two diamond scales. I kept my back to him, and he turned his sky-dark eyes on my mirrored shield, and said "I am sorry, Solna," even as he tried to use my name against me. He cried as I slipped the blade home once, and again, and again, and again, through every chamber of his heart. He cried as his long body writhed in agony, as I came down to hold his head against my bosom and snap his tired neck. The tears soaked through the metal plate and the cotton gambeson and steeped my chest in sagacity and shrewdness, experience and acumen. I wash and wash, but I cannot get it out.

In the town, they hailed me as a savior, offered me fine wines, rich foods, soft beds. Handsome men, pretty women — I refused them all, and in the parlor of the inn they whispered to each other about dedication and purity as I shed my futile armor.

"Send up hot water," I told the landlord, "and keep it coming." Though no water can cleanse me, it's better to try than to despair. A dragon taught me that.

When we were girls, I was the dragon.

"Breathe fire, Solna," Elyndra commanded, and I would roar and cough on all fours, and she would hack off my head.

"Why must you play with that girl?" my mother asked, as if she could not see Elyndra's inborn grace, her golden beauty.

"Because her mother is scullery maid at the castle," my father replied. "And if she did not help us to sell our crop, who would buy it?"

After Vyurfang there was Cold-Heart, whose only weakness was in her mouth, into which I fired an iron quarrel when she spoke of duty and of passion. Her tears are etched into my forearms where I tore the quarrel out so that she would not lie with her mouth open and speechless as her body turned to stone.

And after Cold-Heart, there were Klarsharp, and Windclaw, and Sharpstone, and Zmeyra, and more others than I care to count. Each one marked me with their tears, wrote their passing on my skin. I feel the burden of it like a cloak of chain, slowing my steps, clouding my thoughts. Even when I sleep, it drags me down into nightmare, and when I wake, I force myself to stand only so that I can be doing, not thinking, even if that doing is only a slow march to one more death.

Dragons are a violent breed, with an instinct for survival so deep that even after death, they strive for life. Even while they hope to die, they try to fight. It is an instinct in them, I think, that they cannot suppress. I kill them this way and that way, and every time I think them dead, they twitch and claw and tear. And weep.

"I can't look you in the eye," Elyndra told me when we were older, almost blooded women. "A dragon can enthrall a man with a single glance."

"As you've enthralled Osal," I agreed, making a joke of heartbreak. "Though what you'll do with a thrall so small and weak, I can't say."

"I have you to protect me," she smiled, and kissed me on the cheek. "And Osal is clever, and his father is the glass-smith." But she wouldn't look me in the eye, and her kisses grew fewer as our bodies grew curves.

My armor, once of mirror-shined plate and tight-knit mail is rent now to tatters, discarded across fields and hillsides, caves and plains. Only my weapons remain: a sharp sword, a strong bow, and a promise, burdens now so heavy I can barely walk.

Today, it will end. Today, I will kill my last dragon, or she will kill me. There is always that hope. Today, I go without even my mirror shield to save me from enthralling dragon eyes. I will kill her with my eyes closed, or she will enslave me, or I will die. Today is the end.

They watch me as I go from the village. I have saved a pretty dress for today, a soft cotton gown they gave to me in Hatherton. The canvas baldric pulls against it, pricks the fine weave with coarse fiber until I give up and carry the sword in one hand, arbalest in the other, and the promise on my conscience. I hear the children snicker at a savior in a sun dress, hear parents chide them in quiet, tolerant voices.

I have kept my boots, for the way is muddy, and there are streams I must cross. At the first, I slip the sword under one arm, and pull the dress up to my thighs. It is easier than plate, and more comfortable. The children laugh and point, and make jokes about dragons' legs, but they come no further. We are too close now for childish dares.

It was daring that brought me to this day, and desperation. Desperation to catch the eye of Elyndra, a spare, fine willow to my tall and sturdy walnut. Daring to think she might value strength and commitment over craft or intellect.

When we were women grown, Elyndra went in to the castle, as a lady's under-maid, and I followed her. No lace and fripperies for me, no delicate embroideries on satin underthings, but canvas straps and heavy pikes.

"I'm sorry," Elyndra said when we met in the evenings. "But we must use what we have. I'm pretty. You're strong. Best not to argue with fate." Fate decreed that her mistress invite Olas to show the Countess and court his tricks of glass and wire, and that I enlist as guard trainee.

"You're no nearer Elyndra in the guard than here at home," said my mother when I packed to leave home. "And with your father gone, I need your help."

"I will send my wages," I mumbled.

"Elyndra is a tramp, and a shameless one," said my mother, and she gazed past father's empty chair to the widow Remble's shack. "She'll no more be with you than you'll be a hero, with all your belts and spears and bruises."

The dragon came not long after, a long dark shape like a storm cloud spread thin by wind. It settled on the mountain behind the castle, on the steep slopes that fell off in cliffs to the river below.

"They've written to the Queen," Elyndra said, eyes wide. "They say she'll send a hero! Osal told me so. He said it will be a hero, with landboats so full of armor it'll take ten men to row each one. The Countess herself has ordered him to make a special far-sight device so that she can see the dragon from her tower. And with the pay from it," she looked away, a slight flush across her perfect skin. "Well, you know."

I found a sword easily enough, a rusty piece of steel from the practice racks. Armor I did without, going forth as near-naked then as I do now, though more sensibly dressed in cotton trousers and tunic. I crossed the shallow valley below the castle, went quiet into the dark of the mountains, and climbed through the mist, glad it muffled my scrabbling steps from the dragon whose shadow filled the taprooms.

I found him just above the treeline, in a cave less tunnel than scrape, a shallow overhang of rock exposed to cold winds that fell down from the ice above to the cliff below. I had no mirror, for I was brave, not shrewd, and when he opened his eyes to me, I was lost.

I spent untold centuries in delirious contentment, washed in cerulean tides that hinted love and warmth and certainty until he closed his eyes again and I was free. I wept for loss and fell to my knees to beg him to take me back, my sword discarded dull and evil at my side.

"Have they never told you, girl, to beware a dragon's eyes? Do they not tell tales at night of the cunning of the serpent?" His voice was the slow rumble of an avalanche awakening, and my bones trembled with its might, so that I could not answer. He opened his eyes again, but held back his captivating powers. "Are we so disregarded now, that they send out naked children to do us in? Are you the best there is?"

I told him then, in stumbling, stuttered words of my plan, my hopes, my dreams. Reflected in dragon eyes, Elyndra seemed distant, a slender and a frail reed on which to rest my faith, and I saw clearly now how mad my thoughts had been, how palpable her disinterest in me, how evident her hopes of wealth and position.

"I'm the least there is," I replied as my future fell around me, and I saw in his eyes that even my self-pity was an appeal for deliverance.

"Yet you are the tool I have," he said, "and we must both make do." He snaked his head down from his cave to hang beside me in the chill air. "I cannot give you love," he said. "Though I see you need it, that is the one magic dragons do not have." A lucent tear escaped one lapis eye, and, unthinking, I stretched a hand to touch it. Under my finger, the tear smeared against hard scale, and I felt it enter me, sliding past barriers of skin and flesh to touch my spirit.

"A dragon's tears are potent," he said. "Fools hope to sell them. The wisest know them for a burden, and a shackle." I touched my tear-stained finger to my chest, felt it write destiny on my heart.

"I have no love to give you," he repeated, though I could see in his eyes a love of land and peoples and of me. "I have pain and duty and despondency, and if you want them, they are yours." In that moment, I forsook Elyndra and happiness and hope, and gave myself to fate.

"Our era is done," he said. "The time of dragons and of flight. We have long seen its end arriving. You humans have brought it, with your carts and roads and machines. You have spelled an end to magic with your studies, your scrutiny, your relentless logic."

I thought of the Osal, with his contraptions of wire and melted sand that made my head hurt, and the carter rowing his silly land-boat down dusty roads. I opened my mouth to protest their futility, but the dragon shook his head.

"We have had our time. We have had our peaks and our valleys, our empires and our isolation, our enchantments and our everyday. It is your turn now."

"Our turn for what?" I blurted, mind still full of flight and fantasy.

"For yourselves."

"But why? Stay with us. Guide us." I touched my tear-marked finger to his cold face above the fangs.

"We cannot. Most of us are already gone. Only a few are left — those unaware, or unlucky, and myself, and my queen." He turned his long body and stretched out wings the color of rain-flecked slate that spread out and above me to block the sun. With a snap, he flung them out and down. They crashed against the rock, sending dust and gravel into the icy wind.

When the dust had settled, he spoke again. "These are no more than ornament now. I cannot fly. None of us can, for flight is more magic than mundane. And a dragon that cannot fly is no dragon. Without flight..." I could see the clouds in his eyes, the conflict of desire and memory. "Without flight," he said quietly, "a dragon cannot live. Does not wish to live."

I wept to see him as he saw himself, a master of sky and land reduced to a creeping lizard, wings no more than a hindrance. I wept again as a dragon's true sight showed this to be not self-pity but truth, not despair but acceptance.

"Our instincts are strong," he continued. "Too strong. Those of us who could set them aside have done so. They cast themselves from the heavens while they could still fly, drowned themselves in bitter seas, starved themselves in hidden caverns. They were the lucky ones. The others try, but they fail. They cast themselves from cliffs too low to kill, topple boulders they can dislodge at need, challenge champions they cannot help but battle against. They are broken in body and in spirit, but dragon bodies heal even when the spirit cannot. And yet they try, failing over and over again, and achieving only pain."

I looked about me. Fine dust had settled on the dragon's useless wings, torn and crumpled at the tips where they had struck the rock, and leaking drops of emerald blood onto soil from which sprang moss and fern. Beside me, my discarded sword mocked my brash ignorance. I pulled my courage about me as best I could. "Let me help," I said, as if a foolish girl with a rusty sword were of some value.

Wisdom is not kindness, and truth is not comfort. I saw, through his eyes and my own, how unequal I was to the offer I made, how much he would have preferred a more accomplished servant, how little choice he had. I saw his dismay at my inadequacy, his determination to exceed it.

"You are not the tool I hoped for," he admitted. "Yet my queen set me to wait here among the humans, and you are the one who has come. We must make the best of it. In the face of failure, we cannot succeed if we do not try."

We agreed then, how I would search out his fellows, and kill them despite themselves. He gave me a small sack of gems from the small hoard he had carried, taught me how to use a mirror, how to find a dragon's weak points, how best to use them, and how to be sure of death.

"These are the secrets of the ancients," he rumbled, laughing. "For centuries, we have kept them from you humans, and now I show you freely the chinks in my armor. It is," he bared his fangs, "a bitter irony."

When we had done, and I had memorized and practiced and repeated to his satisfaction, night was well upon us.

"Come and sleep under my wing," he said, "and tomorrow we will finish."

Had any human ever slept with a dragon? I wondered, as I snuggled close against the fine scales with their scent of oats and pepper.

"You are the first," he answered. "The last. The only."

In the morning, I watched as he he flung himself from the cliff, and fell, and soared for one last moment, like leaves of autumn gold defiant in the sun. And then I climbed down to his broken, bloody body to wipe away his last tears and cut off his head.

I took them with into town — the tears invisibly traced across my palms, the head across broad shoulders, with flowers springing up in my path where emerald blood had trickled down my back and legs into the soil. I felt my body stronger and harder than I had ever known it, and my heart more desolate.

I delivered the head to the Countess, and she gave me honor, gold, and armor. All went as the dragon had predicted. 'The dragon,' I called him, for only now did I realize that I had never learned his name, and because the humans did not care. They looked at me, with my dragon-marked skin, and looked away.

I set off to the next town afoot, spurning the carter and his land-boat. Only as I left did I think to look for Elyndra. I found her, in her cotton dress that shone like satin, saw her wide-eyed fear as she stood next to Osal for protection against the horror and hero I had become.

I am still the horror. I kill noble, beautiful creatures when they are weak and defenseless. The map of tears across my body has grown so heavy now that only my sword keeps me upright. I dull its sharp point, stabbing it into the stone of the mountain as I climb. At the last narrow scramble, the arbalest grew too heavy, and I left it beside the path for some foolish child to find. It is hard to care about the humans now that I have seen so many in so much foolishness. They celebrate the death of dragons as if it were an accomplishment. If that is their future, they deserve it.

I can sense the last one near me now, smell her pepper scent around a ridge of jagged rock This the queen, of course. The last dragon. The last of my burdens, of my impossible task. I put down my sword to tug my gown straight, brush the burrs from its hem. It is tight at the waist and shoulders, and it leaves my arms naked to the wind, but it is the best I have, the only good thing I have.

I leave my sword where it lies. In a queen, the instinct for survival may be stronger. She may kill me on sight — sear me and my pretty dress with a breath of fire, or rend me with her fangs. I can hope.

I step out around the ridge. She is vast, this queen, the size of houses. Her scales are violet and indigo and blue and black in the autumn sun, and her wings form caverns across the slanted meadow. Her eyes are the green of forests and rain. I lean my spirit toward them … and do not fall.

"You are proof against us now, child," she says, but I have enough dragon in me now to know it for a joke, to know that she holds back her power.

"I cannot kill you," I say, letting my shoulders slump. Let there be an end to death at last. My arms are cold, and the dress does little to warm the rest of me.

"There is no need," she replies, and rests her head beside me on the ground.

"I cannot kill you," I insist. "I will not kill you. I have done enough." I look up to her forest eyes, and beg them for release. "Let me rest. Let me finish." We both know what I mean.

"We have used you hard," she admits. "We have been unfair, even cruel." I see the truth of it in her gaze.

We are silent for a time. "He used his power," I realize at last, and know it true. "It was not my choice. All this killing. All this death."

I think back on all the bodies, the blood. I feel the tracery of tears burn across my hands, my chest, my back. Not bravely, freely chosen. Not voluntary service to a dying race, but an unwitting tool — a fool of death.

I sit, and wait for my own tears to flow, to fill the hollow of my disillusion.

"He could not help it," she says at last. "It is the way of dragons, to control, to master, to deceive."

"To enslave," I spit, though I cannot muster anger.

"Yes. Yet our time is ended. Your technology drains the world of magic, but it is your will that prevails — that indomitable will that fights tyranny, resists oppression."

She smiles her dragon smile, all fangs and sharp eyes. "Even you, little one. Not the strongest of your race, nor the best. But even you have come this morning to refuse me. Thus we reach our end, when an unarmed young human denies a dragon queen."

"I will not kill you," I say again, bitter now with the knowledge that I have been used, that I am as poor a vessel as I once feared — that I was chosen for my very weakness. Relief grows in me as well; I am done forever with that task, done with blood, done with dragons and their deaths.

"No other could have done it. Strong, determined, implacable. Enthralled." She shows me the truth of it, shows me her gratitude. Perhaps I have done well. Perhaps not. Perhaps I am only tired. Whatever the truth, I want no more of it.

"I will not kill you," I say a fourth time.

"Even a timeworn dragon queen is a queen." She shakes her wings, and a breeze blows through my hair. "I have one more flight left in me, and I will take it until it ends. But we owe you thanks, we dragons. What boon can I give you, who have given us so much?"

"Death and blood," I say, for that is what I have given. What I was forced to give.

"Dignity," she replies. "And for a dragon, that is a great deal."

I am dull now, with disillusion. I want no more revelations, no boons. I want ... I do not know, and I sit in silence, my pretty, foolish dress a dusty folly, poor shield against the mountain cold. I want no more killing, no more effort, no more decisions, no more plans. No more weapons. No more tears. Above all, no more tears.

"Take me with you." On that final flight, the last voyage of the last dragon.

She looks at me, forest eyes impenetrable as oak.

"Very well," she agrees, and her eyes glint with moisture.

She gathers me into one huge paw, and I see the razor claws pressing into her scales as she stretches them to keep me safe. It hurts her, but I do not care. Why should I be the only one to hurt? And if she slips, and the claws close in, what matter? The dragon tears on my skin reproach me, show me the child that I am acting. I tell them silently to let me die as a I choose, and they do not argue with my wisdom, little as it is.

We rise with a clap of thunder and a rush of wind, and then we are high above the land, and in the village below, the humans run like raindrops, away, away, away.

We fly over the land I have known all my life, over the sites of my bloody executioner's work, and of my birth and childhood. It is small, inconsequential, the sites of my great and awful deeds a tiny patch of green and brown upon the great sprawl of land and sea beneath us. There is too much of it! The mountain I climbed this morning, no more than a foothill for a range of granite peaks, with beyond them the glint of water. We follow rivers to the west, and I silently urge the queen on, further, faster, to see more before the end.

She slithers her head down to me like a goose, so that she is flying one way, facing the other, then turns her head back toward the front, her long neck forming a loop that ends above my head. "There are lands below even the bards have not heard of, lands where dragons and their deaths are a matter of legend," she says through the wind of her passage. "There are lands that speak different tongues, even between humans. Lands of carters and craft, lands of farmers and hard work, lands of battle and lands of peace, lands of beauty and of plainness."

"This is what we give you," she says, and I feel her wingbeats falter. "These were our lands, that now are yours." We slip in the air as the magic fades and I sense her muscles straining.

We sink lower and lower, and my heart aches for all the lands I have not seen, the magic of horizon and discovery. Soon, the flight must end, and the queen and I will reach the end of our voyage, and the beginning of peace.

We are hilltop-high now, above a green land of forests and rain and ocean. "This was my favorite," she says, and there is regret in the soughing of her voice. "Here I was my happiest." She swoops low over the waves on a warm, sandy beach, and I feel her tears bathing my body as her claws shift and the end nears. I close my eyes, and feel her joy and sorrow as she remembers happiness and her race dies. "I hope there is room for me in your Atlas," she says. Then the claws open, and I am falling, falling, into the waves.

I strike hard, and the breath whooshes out of me and the cold green is all around me, and I am sorry. I kick out for the surface, and the air, and as my head breaks through, I see a dark arrowhead against the sky, climbing, climbing out to sea. And then it falls.

It's better to try than to despair. A dragon taught me that. I hold the lesson close as a current carries me to an uncharted shore of hope and life, and the salt water washes me clean.

About the story

I'm a big fan of Deep Purple, and of many of its component members, including the late Jon Lord (keyboards). I was listening to his album *Pictured Within* early one morning after dropping my spouse off at the airport. The title song is beautiful, but it includes the line "There are dragons I have slain". It works in the song, but as a long-time vegan, I was a little uncomfortable singing along.

That moral discomfort led me to a search for circumstances in which I could sing the line in good conscience. The opening line of the story came to me almost immediately, and I had the whole thing mapped out, and the first paragraphs crafted, by the time I got home ten minutes later. I wrote the story that same morning.

About the Author

B. Morris Allen is a biochemist turned activist turned lawyer turned foreign aid consultant, and frequently wonders whether it's time for a new career. He's been traveling since birth, and has lived on five of seven continents. When he can, he makes his home on the Oregon coast. In between journeys, he edits Metaphorosis magazine, and works on his own speculative stories of love and disaster. His dark fantasy novel *Susurrus* came out in 2017.

You can find him at BMorrisAllen.com, on Twitter @BMorrisAllen, and occasionally on Facebook at Facebook.com/BmorrisAllen.

Copyright

Title information

Chambers of the Heart

ISBN: 978-1-64076-518-4 (e-book)
ISBN: 978-1-64076-519-1 (paperback)
ISBN: 978-1-64076-520-7 (hardcover)

Copyright

First appearance

"Chambers of the Heart" was first published in *Metaphorosis* on Friday, 24 February 2017.

"Building on Sand" was first published in *Kaleidotrope* on Monday, 1 July 2019.

"Blush" was first published in *Capricious* on Monday, 29 May 2017.

"Minstrel Boy Howling at the Moon" was first published in *The Magazine of Fantasy & Science Fiction* on Monday, 1 March 2021.

"Fetch" was first published in *Metaphorosis* on Friday, 4 September 2020.

"The Humblebract Expedition" was first published in the anthology *Score* on Sunday, 24 February 2019.

"When Dooryards First in the Lilac Bloomed" was first published in *Lackington's* on Wednesday, 24 May 2017.

"Some Sun and Delilah" was first published in *Metaphorosis* on Friday, 6 September 2019.

"Crying in the Salt House" was first published in *Cirsova* on Thursday, 22 November 2018.

"Full of Stars" was first published in *Stargazers* on Friday, 23 October 2020.

"Memory and Faded Ink" was first published in *Aurealis* on Wednesday, 10 July 2019.
"Fountainhead" was first published in the anthology *Score* on Sunday, 24 February 2019.
"Adaptations to Coastal Erosion" was first published in *Metaphorosis* on Friday, 24 June 2016.
"Outburst" was first published in *Cast of Wonders* on Monday, 29 May 2017.
"The Irrigation Ditch" was first published in the anthology *Shards* on Monday, 1 October 2018.
"Dragons I Have Slain" was first published in *Metaphorosis* on Friday, 2 September 2016.

Works of fiction

All rights reserved

Moral rights asserted

Publisher

Plant Based Press is an imprint of
Metaphorosis Publishing
Neskowin, OR, USA

www.metaphorosis.com

"Metaphorosis" is a registered trademark.

Discounts available

Metaphorosis Publishing

Metaphorosis offers beautifully written science fiction and fantasy. Our imprints include:

Metaphorosis Magazine

Plant Based Press

Verdage

Vestige

Help keep Metaphorosis running at
Patreon.com/metaphorosis

See more about some of our books on the following pages.

Metaphorosis

a magazine of speculative fiction

Metaphorosis is an online speculative fiction magazine dedicated to quality writing. We publish an original story every week, along with author bios, interviews, and notes on story origins. Come and see us online at magazine.Metaphorosis.com

Keep Metaphorosis running! Support us at
Patreon.com/metaphorosis

You can also find us at:
Twitter: @MetaphorosisMag, @MetaphorosisRev,
@Metaphorosis
Facebook: www.facebook.com/metaphorosis

We publish monthly print and e-book issues, as well as yearly Best of and Complete anthologies.

Vegan-friendly science fiction and fantasy, including an annual anthology of the year's best SFF stories.

Susurrus

A darkly romantic story of magic, love, and suffering.

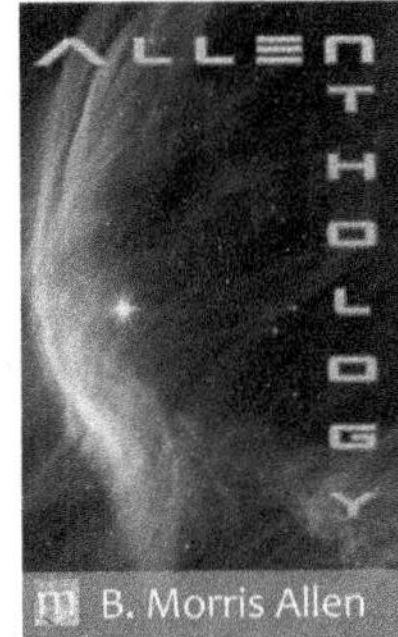

Allenthology: Volume I

A quarter century of SFF from B. Morris Allen, including the full contents of the collections *Tocsin, Start with Stones,* and *Metaphorosis.*

Best Vegan Science Fiction & Fantasy
2016-2020

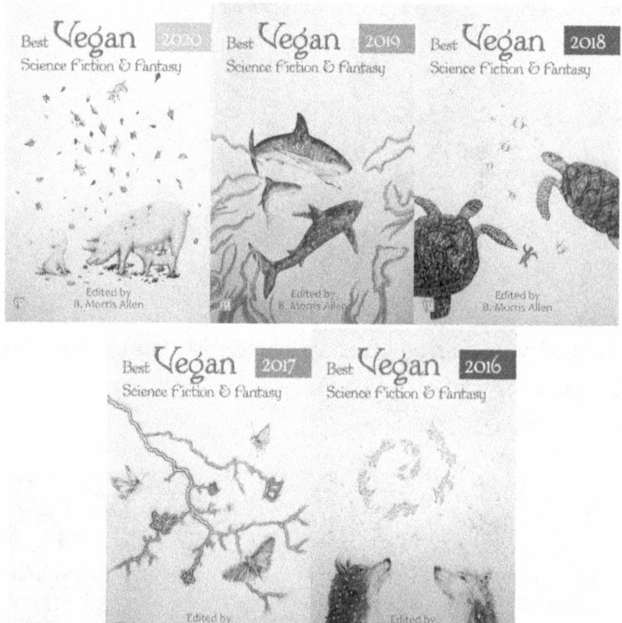

The best vegan-friendly science fiction and fantasy stories from each year. Great SFF that just doesn't happen to include meat-eating, hunting, horse-riding, etc.

Verdage

Science fiction and fantasy books for writers – full of great stories, but with an additional focus on the craft of speculative fiction writing.

Reading 5X5 x2

Duets

How do authors' voices change when they collaborate?

A round-robin of five talented science fiction and fantasy authors collaborating with each other and writing solo.

Including stories by Evan Marcroft, David Gallay, J. Tynan Burke, L'Erin Ogle, and Douglas Anstruther.

Score

an SFF symphony

What if stories were written like music? *Score* is an anthology of varied stories arranged to follow an emotional score from the heights of joy to the depths of despair – but always with a little hope shining through.

Reading 5X5

Five stories, five times

Twenty-five SFF authors, five base stories, five versions of each – see how different writers take on the same material, with stories in contemporary and high fantasy, soft and hard SF, and a mysterious 'other' category.

Reading 5X5

Writers' Edition

All the stories from the regular, readers' edition, plus two extra stories, the story seed, and authors' notes on writing. Over 100 pages of additional material specifically aimed at writers.

Vestige

Novelettes, novellas, and novels by Metaphorosis authors.

The Nocturnals
Mariah Montoya

Night is Dangerous. Day is deadly.

Where day and night last thirty years, humans move constantly stay ahead of the night and cruel Nocturnals that call it home. But now a boy is lost out there.